SCHUTZSTAFFEL RISING

CHAIN OF DECEIT, BOOK 6

By D.A. McIntosh

Schutzstaffel

[shoo ts-shtah-fuh l]
noun, German.

They were an elite military unit of the Nazi party that served as
Hitler's bodyguard and as a special police force.
The internal security force of Nazi Germany, 1930, literally
"defense squadron."
>   Better known by its initials, **SS**

Source: Online Etymology Dictionary, © 2010 Douglas Harper

SCHUTZSTAFFEL RISING
Chain of Deceit Book 6

Special thanks to the following for assistance and encouragement in completion of this book and my previous books. There are more to come and they support me by adding quality comments, technical support and suggestions. Thanks to Carol, my wife, Tony and Cynthia, and a support group that is growing daily.

This novel is dedicated to all the men and women who have served or are serving in our Armed Forces defending our nation from enemies both foreign and domestic. To those who have given some and especially to those who gave it all. Without those we would not be a free country. Also a special thanks to the men and women of our nations police and Fire Departments, who without their protection, dedication and trust we would fall as a nation. Thank you for your dedication.
Freedom is not free.

Other Novels by D.A. McIntosh

The Chain of Deceit series

Chain of Deceit, Book 1
Retribution, Book 2
T-Minus 36, Book 3
Final Report, Book 4
Wounded Eagle, Book 5

CHARACTERS

Davin Pierce – Assistant Director CIA Covert Operations

Josh Randal – Director CIA Covert Operations

Stephanie Randal – CIA Agent

Connie Pierce – FBI Agent

Joanne Morgan – CIA Agent aka Mi-Cha Sang

President of the United States - Darrell Mitchell

National Security Advisor - Tony Sanford

Director CIA - Ms Ashley Peterson

Hans Bormann – German Citizen

Gregory Dietrich – Billionaire German Citizen

Michelle Dietrich – Sister of Gregory Dietrich

Rafael Jordan – CIA Agent

Season Garcia – CIA Agent

John Polson – Section chief, White House Secret Service

Amber Miller – Secret Service Agent

Captain Steve Blair – Pilot of CIA Gulfstream

Mary – Stewardess on CIA Gulfstream and field operative

General Soon-Bok Kim – Commander of North Korean Secret Police

General Jin-Ho Shin - Launched ICBMs at America

Lt. Commander Price – Seal Team Six commander

Doctor Dobrinski – President's personal White House doctor

Michael Bell – Vice President of the United States

Henry – Copilot of CIA Gulfstream

Brian – CIA Team 2 Lead

Colonel Max Griffin – Commander US Army Forces

Major General Lester Pride – Commander Joint Task Forces, Washington D.C.

TABLE OF CONTENTS

Prologue - Recap of *Wounded Eagle*

The country was a mess; Boston and Denver were recovering from nuclear devastation. Many cities were still recovering from terrorist attacks, total infrastructure failure, power outages, riots, gang wars and martial law. The attack on Washington D.C. by the North Koreans was almost a success. Unfortunately, their attack on McDill Air Force Base was a success. United States Air Force Cyber Command lost several good technicians who were attempting to repair the infrastructure that had been taken down by cyber terrorists.

President Mitchell was back in the White House but had to evacuate to Mount Weather on several occasions to ensure the government was still mostly intact. His daughter had been kidnapped and rescued by Josh Randal, Senior CIA Field Operative. Davin Pierce was severely injured while tracking down the German terrorist Hans Bormann when his wife, Connie, and he were kidnapped by Bormann.

Josh was promoted to Director of Covert Operations for the CIA and Davin became the Assistant Director for Covert Operations. Life could not be better until they were both called upon to capture the man that caused most of the destruction within the country. Hans Bormann had escaped while being transferred to Washington for trial. They were tasked to find him and make sure he did not return to cause anymore damage. This was to be a black operation, a specialty of the Covert Operations Division of the CIA. An operation that would not be recorded anywhere and only a few would know the operation ever happened. Davin and Josh would take lead on this and only bring in handpicked field agents to assist.

The following story never happened, according to the CIA, the United States of America government, FBI, or any government agency.

America had been kicked in *Wounded Eagle* and would be kicked even harder in *Schutzstaffel Rising*. It wasn't over yet.

Chapter 1 New Life

The waiting is always the hardest part for both parents. Connie wanted the pain to end, and Davin was just worried. Davin lived his life on his terms and had not worried about anyone other than Connie for the past couple of years. She was a trained FBI agent and very capable in her own right. But this was different, nature was taking over; child birth was different for every woman and man. Some women had an easy birth, others not so. The men in their lives were a different story; some worried for no reason, and others felt that nature and good doctors would handle all of it. And, to top it off, he had never really been good around children and now he was about to be a father. They had been at the hospital for three hours and still no baby.

"Josh, Stephanie, I do appreciate you two being here, but I know you both have work to do and this is just taking too long," Davin said trying to break the ice in the room.

"Yes, we both have work that we should be doing, but this is as important to us as it is to you. We will stick around until…" Stephanie stated but was interrupted when the nurse walked in and announced, "Mr. Pierce and friends would you please come with me to meet your new family." Realizing she had interrupted Stephanie, "Oh, sorry, but I believe you have been waiting for me. Now please follow me."

Minutes later, they entered Connie's room only to stop and stare at Connie and the two small bundles she was holding.

"Holy cow, two, it can't be!" Davin exclaimed. He seemed surprised at what he saw as he walked over to her bed. "Wow, Connie are you okay?"

"I am doing fine, honey. I would like to introduce you to our new family; we have to name them soon so the doctor can fill out the birth certificates properly," she replied with a smile and chuckle, thinking about how Davin got his name. His mother wanted David and his dad wanted to call him Kevin and the doctor started writing David and ended up writing an 'n' at the end of David giving him the name Davin. It had never been changed; and he had been Davin since birth, because of a mistake that was not caught until the certificate had been filed.

"What do you think of Joshua David for your parents and your best friend, and Amber Marie for mine?" Connie asked. "I think those will work just fine."

"Well Davin, ole buddy, I guess your nights are going to be full of dirty diapers and lack of sleep. Do you want a cot set up in your office so you can get some sleep?" Josh joked.

"Not yet, say hi to Josh and Amber," Davin said as he picked up one of the babies. "Who do I have here?"

"That is your son, can't you tell the difference?" Connie stated. "And this is Amber with the wavy hair."

"Hello," Josh said into his cell letting it ring only once. "Sorry, I have to take this," he said and walked out of the room, returning minutes later not looking very happy.

"What is it, Josh?" Davin asked.

"Stephanie, stay here with Connie. I need to take Davin back to the office; we have a situation," Josh commented.

"Sorry, honey, duty calls; and when he calls I have to run. I will be back as soon as I can," Davin said and handed Josh to Stephanie.

CIA Headquarters, Langley, Virginia

"Who do we have?" Josh asked his secretary as he and Davin walked into his outer office.

"You have visitors in your office and they are not very happy," she replied, and then glanced over at the side of the wall to view three Secret Service Agents sitting comfortably in the brown overstuffed chairs provided for waiting guests. One was reading a current copy of *Newsweek* and the other two just looked bored.

"Who?" Josh asked. He looked at the two men and one woman sitting in the chairs, and then realized who was in the office and said to himself, *'Oh hell.'*

"President Mitchell," she answered seeing that he figured it out himself, "Should I bring coffee or anything?"

"No, that's okay; Davin, what do you think he wants? Yes, get some coffee and water," he replied and then changed his mind as he opened the door and entered Josh's office. "Mr. President and Mr. Sanford what brings you down to our humble office?"

"We have something to discuss with the CIA; Ms Peterson will be here in a minute," Tony Sanford, National Security Advisor stated as he took a seat beside the President. Just then Ashley Peterson, CIA Director stepped into the office.

"Good morning gentlemen, sorry I am late, traffic," she commented and shook the hands of each member present.

"Please take a seat, Ms Peterson. We have a problem," President Darrell Mitchell said as she walked in.

"Comes with the territory, sir. What have you got?" Josh asked as he walked around behind his desk and sat. "Georgia is bringing in some refreshments, so if you want to wait, she…"

"She has clearance, right?" Sanford asked.

"Yes, equal to mine and Davin's," Josh reported.

"Then please take a seat; this is not going to set well with any of you. Do you want to tell them, sir?" Sanford asked as he looked at Mitchell.

"No, go on, you tell them," Mitchell ordered.

"Okay, sir. We got this early this morning. It was in the morning mail," Sanford started, and handed a copy of the letter to Ashley, Josh and Davin. "Please read and hand back, immediately."

"Why now?" Davin asked.

"Now, because we are still in the process of recovery and still very vulnerable," Mitchell commented. "What do you think; do you believe he can pull it off?"

"Well, we do know that Bormann has some very high placed people with a lot of money backing him; so if anyone can, then he can," Josh stated looking very concerned.

"But seriously sir, this letter means nothing; anyone can send you a letter stating that we lost and he will return and this time he will succeed. How many death threats do you get? Every president gets death threats and only a few have actually been assassinated although there were a couple of close calls a few other times," Mitchell stated.

"But this Bormann kidnapped your daughter and Mrs. Pierce, attempted to kill Mr. Pierce, and we have yet to prove he was involved in the deaths of several low lives like the 'Weasel' in San Francisco and a couple of others from the Guzman drug cartel," Sanford commented, looking a little disturbed.

"What's your point? We know the guy is bad, so does that mean he is or isn't going to attempt to kill me and who knows how many of our civilians," Mitchell argued. "Randal, read that letter and you tell me what you think."

"I have read it, sir; and it looks very much like Mr. Bormann has revived the Nazi party and is set on destroying you and this country. He does mention in this line, and I quote, 'We will not lose; we have the manpower, the weapons and resolve to bring your country to its knees.' According to Adolf Hitler, they were on a quest, a religious quest, to eliminate all those that opposed them. And his spiritual leader, Reichsfuhrer-SS Heinrich Himmler established the elite police force known as the Schutzstaffel, SS as they were well known, and advised Hitler on everything including the scriptures. A recent show on the *Discovery* channel talked about the Nazi Gospel and how they were destined to rule the world," Josh summarized.

"They what?" Mitchell asked.

"It really gets deeper than that; history as taught in our schools about the Nazis is a little behind the curve. They were very nasty people, brain washed from a young age, thinking that the Aryan was the super race and all non-Aryans were denied many rights and privileges that the super race had. That was the start of the first race-based laws," Davin added. "I studied and researched the Third Reich in college and it has been a pet project of mine over the years."

"No sir, it means we need to take this seriously. We know that Mr. Randal and Pierce have good reason to go after this guy. Let me ask, Randal, Pierce, do you have any idea as to the location of Bormann or the money he is being financed with?" Sanford asked looking at the two Covert Operations men in charge.

"Sir, yes, we have been using all our resources to locate this scumbag; but just when we think we are close, we run into a brick wall. Our last known location is GITMO; and then, when he was being transported to D.C. for trial, he escaped. It was well planned and executed. Two officers were injured but are back on duty. From there we were able to track him to Columbia and lost him there. We know he has connections with several drug cartels and political higher ups so he was able to disappear. We have hit more road blocks than we can count."

"With Ms Peterson's blessing and resources we want you to turn up the heat," Mitchell stated. "This country has endured enough from those people, Nazis or not. I am about to give you an order that technically I can't; but in this room, right now, I will. Turn up the heat, locate Bormann and whoever is financing him and kill them. Take no prisoners. And if we need to send the military, I will. Understand?"

"We will handle it personally, sir," Josh said in agreement and then looked over at Davin and Ashley, getting a nod from each of them. "And as far as the military, put them on standby. We may need them to take care of his army. We may still have World War III on the horizon."

Chapter 2 Korean Connection

CIA office of Covert Operations

"Josh, I just received a very interesting call from Joanne in Korea," Davin Pierce, Assistant Director Covert Operations, responsible for handling the Eastern field agents, said as he entered Josh's office.

"What does Mi-Cha Sang have to say?" Josh Randal, Director of Covert Operations, responsible for Western operations, asked, referring to Joanne Morgan's Korean cover name, the one she used while undercover or in country.

"She found out that a rogue general received a large sum of money from an off-shore account. He was paid to launch those ICBMs. She has a name and is working on getting a location. I asked our research department to provide me with a background on him; they should have that information in a few hours. Joanne said she will have that location in a few days and then she will move in to handle him," Davin reported.

"Will she report in before she does anything?" Josh asked.

"Yes, she knows the rules, no arrest or removal before getting permission," Davin replied.

"Good, now let's move on to our new assignment. Have you got time?"

"Yes, but first, we just received an update on the death toll and it isn't good; radiation sickness has claimed more."

"All the more reason to get these guys…," Josh started to say but was interrupted by his intercom buzzing; he turned and pressed the intercom button. "Yes."

"Stephanie is here to see you, sir."

"Good, send her in," he said and then stood to greet his wife, who had recently graduated from the academy at the farm. As she entered, Josh walked over, kissed her and asked her to take a seat. "We need your help on this assignment."

"Stephanie, Davin and I have been given an assignment that will put us in harm's way again. You are not to do anything without mine or Davin's permission. Do you understand?"

"Yes, I understand, but don't understand why you have to say that."

"Because, honey, sometimes you get a little headstrong and go off on your own. I know how you are. Now we have been tasked to locate and destroy Hans Bormann and whoever is financing him."

"What?" Stephanie exclaimed.

"We have been tasked to kill Bormann and destroy his army," Davin restated.

"Okay, I will shut up and listen," Stephanie said but then continued, "Davin how are Connie and the kids doing?"

"They are doing fine; came home yesterday. You need to stop by and see them as soon as you can."

"Thanks," she replied and then she shut up.

"Davin, Bormann's last known location is Columbia and I guess that is where we need to start. I have already tasked our agents down there to kick over some stones and see what they can come up with. So far we have nothing."

"I will get the company jet from Ashley and we can leave in the morning. I want one night with my new family before we go off and get killed," Davin said smiling.

"Don't say that, Davin. You are not going to get killed," Stephanie almost yelled at him.

"That, of course, is not my plan; but as I used to tell my troops when I was in the army, 'Let the enemy die for his country, you live for yours'."

"Yep, just like Butch Cassidy and the Sundance Kid, go down to Columbia and face off a bunch of Columbian soldiers; well, in this case, a bunch of Nazis," Josh joked.

"They went to Bolivia, not Columbia. And am I Butch or Sundance?" Davin replied correcting Josh's minor mistake about the history of Butch Cassidy and the Sundance Kid.

"You're Sundance; I am the good looking one. And you are better with your gun, just like Sundance," Josh acknowledged; and without skipping a beat, he continued directing his words to Stephanie. "Honey, I need you here to coordinate with Ashley while we are gone. I will call as much as I can on a secure line. So keep your SAT phone with you at all times. Our cover names will be Butch and Sundance for this op. And it will be unofficially known as *Operation Sundance.*"

"Okay, Butch, let's get some lunch before you two go out with a bang," Stephanie said as she stood and grabbed for Josh's hand. He reached into his desk drawer and pulled out his weapon.

"Let's go; I could use a good burger and a pile of fries. Are you coming Davin?" Josh asked.

"No, got a bit of work to complete before leaving. And I want to go home early. I will grab something from the café," Davin responded.

The next morning they boarded the company Gulfstream and headed south to Columbia.

Berlin, Germany, same day

Gregory 'Sepp' Dietrich was sitting at his desk considering his next move. His sister had survived the accident, so he changed his mind; instead of killing her, he planned on sending her to Hollywood.

"Hello, this is Dietrich," he said into the phone after letting it ring three times. "Hans, where are you?"

"I am in Columbia; arrived here a week ago. I am working with some old friends to get a flight out in the morning. Did the letter get sent to the President?" Hans Bormann asked.

"Yes, they should have gotten it yesterday. All hell is going to break soon, so you better get back here as soon as possible. They are probably monitoring all calls from Colombia so we need to end this. Get here as fast as possible, we are about to begin," Dietrich said and then hung up.

US Embassy, Bogotá, Columbia

Behind a locked door more was happening in the Office of South American Affairs than just coordination of the Ambassador's schedule. They handled that in the outer office; however, behind the secretary was a door that looked like any other door in the facility, but was, in fact, a camouflaged vault door. The secretary was actually an armed guard, highly trained in hand to hand combat and weapons. She looked and acted like any other secretary, as a sweet middle-aged woman who would hide in the event of an attack. But she would not hide; like firemen, she would run into the fire and defend to the death, preferably of the attacker not her own. Attached to the desk were two weapons, a 12 gauge automatic shotgun and her favorite handgun, a 15 round Berretta 92F. She also carried a Berretta compact at all times, hidden on the small of her back. Dressed in a simple black suit, with the skirt a little shorter than normally allowed, enabled her to move quicker to defend herself. A white blouse and black jacket finished her appearance and covered her small automatic.

Behind the vault door was a collection of electronic equipment designed to intercept all sorts of communication signals, from cell phone to radio transmissions. This was not unusual; every nation, whether it be a government or news outlets on the planet monitored other countries' communications. What were they looking for? The answer to that was the same for all those monitoring stations. They wanted something to exploit, write a damaging article about, or follow a trail of money or persons of interest.

"Sir, that call you have been asking about, just happened," the operator said to his section chief when he saw her walk into the control room.

"Did you get a location?" she asked quickly.

"No, call was too short; but we were able to narrow it down to Columbia."

"What did he say?" the chief asked, and after getting the gist of the conversation she said, "I will pass it on to Butch and Sundance. Keep monitoring that line and get me a location, top priority," the chief ordered and then headed for the door.

"Roger that, sir."

"She expects miracles and we are fresh out of them today," he said after she left the room, "We can't provide something that we can't monitor. Maybe we should get some field agents to go out and do some real collection, the old fashion way, talking to other humans."

"You know that isn't going to happen, boss. With all the stuff going on back home, they are not spending the money to do HUMINT," one of his operators commented, referring to the collection of Human Intelligence.

"Yeah, I know, Bates; get back to work, don't you have someone to track?"

"Yeah, yeah, I know, the mission, the fricken mission. I will be glad when my tour of duty is up down here. I hate this place and the beer sucks too."

"Quit complaining, it could be worse."

"How so, my commander, how so?"

"You could be in Afghanistan."

"There is that, I guess. But at least there I would see some action," he complained.

"Get back to work," he replied and then turned to leave.

"Wait, that number just came up again."

After listening for a couple of minutes and getting a positive trace on it, they had a location. The shift boss took it and ran out of the room, heading to catch the director.

"Sarah, ahh, Ms Director, we have a location and a way in. He ordered a charter flight to leave in an hour. Should we send in a team?"

"No. We wait for the A team. We don't have the resources to take him."

Chapter 3 Missed by That Much!

Davin and Josh's Gulfstream landed at El Nuevo Dorado International Airport at 11:15 a.m. on a beautiful Columbian morning. After leaving the runway, they taxied to CATAM (Cundianmarca Columbia Military Base) located in the center of the airfield. Their arrival had been coordinated by Ms Peterson and the base commander. He had agreed to support the CIA in their quest to capture Hans Bormann, providing troops and equipment as needed.

Unknown to Davin and Josh at the time, only three hundred yards northwest of the military base was the General Aviation terminal where Hans Bormann was boarding a chartered aircraft.

Davin and Josh were walking down the stairway from the corporate jet and greeted by Agents Rafael Jordan, Season Garcia and General Jaime Moreno in Bogotá, Colombia. They did not have a plan other than meeting with their connection in Bogotá and going from there.

"Good morning, Mr. Randal and Mr. Pierce, this is General Moreno and my partner Season Garcia. Welcome to

Columbia," Agent Jordan said as Davin and Josh came down the stairs.

"Pleasure to meet you," Josh said shaking the hands of the General and Garcia. "Is there a place we can talk?"

"Yes Mr. Randal, my office is secure; come with me," General Moreno answered and then turned and signaled to his two Captains to move.

Ten minutes later, the group was sitting around a large solid wood conference table with refreshments in front of each of them.

"General, I assume Ms Peterson briefed you on our mission?" Davin asked before taking a sip from his water.

"Yes, Ms Peterson asked for my assistance in the capture of a Hans Bormann. We are a non-extradition country as you know. But when she explained what this Bormann has done and is planning on doing, I have to agree that he should be removed from my country. If he has plans on destroying your country, he may want to expand into others, including mine. And I cannot have that. We have our problems with the drug cartels and crime, and we cannot have men like Mr. Bormann running around my country creating more problems. What is it that you need from me, Mr. Randal?"

"On our plane, we have a team of experts that are with us to assist in his removal. They speak your language, as we do, and will be dressed similar to your special weapons teams. We would like you to give us a squad of your best to assist, preferably sniper qualified. They need to follow our orders without question; and once we have finished here, they are not to discuss what happened to anyone. Is that possible, sir?"

"Yes, I will have Captain Martinez, and five of his best, join you after you leave this office. I will also provide you with an office in the corner of the hanger to run your operation. Captain Martinez will help you set up there."

"Just before we landed, we received information as to where Bormann was; but that was an hour ago. He may have left already, but that will be our first stop," Josh stated.

Charter Flight 589 to Austria

"This is your captain on the flight deck; we are climbing to eight thousand feet as we leave Columbian airspace. Please sit back and enjoy the ride; we will be in Panama shortly," the pilot reported. "And thank you for flying Panama Air Charters. You can earn frequent flyer miles for every trip, good for free stuff at the gift shop."

Bormann's flight to Panama was uneventful and short. After landing, he walked over to the terminal to check in with the Charter flight service he had booked with before leaving Columbia. After checking in, he was told they could depart immediately if he was ready. He boarded the corporate jet that was waiting on the tarmac and took a seat in an overstuffed lounge chair midway down the cabin.

"Welcome aboard, Mr. Jacobs. Would you care for a drink before we take off?" the steward asked Hans Bormann; she did not know his true identity. Since Bormann was flying on a fake passport and identity, he had been able to charter the business jet for the Trans Atlantic flight with the help of a friend. He was also a life member of the Nazi movement within which Bormann was designated a SS- Obergruppenfuhrer und General der Waffen-SS. (SS-Senior group leader and general of the Waffen-SS). He reported directly to SS-Oberst-Gruppenfuhrer und Generaloberst der Waffen-SS (SS-Supreme group leader and colonel general of the Waffen-SS) Gregory 'Sepp' Dietrich. Dietrich would have reported directly to Adolf Hitler if he were still alive.

"Yes, red wine please," he responded and then glanced out the window from his comfortable seat.

"Dinner will be served shortly; would you prefer steak or chicken?"

"Steak, please, medium well," Bormann replied and returned his gaze out the window at the country rapidly flowing below the plane until they entered a cloud.

"Yes, sir, I'll be right back with your wine," she said and then turned and headed back to the galley. Bormann was the only one on the plane besides the pilots and steward. He liked it that way, no witnesses to his escape from Columbia, which is why he had chartered a small twin engine to fly him to Panama where he would be able to link up with the chartered jet waiting for his arrival.

So far the flight was uneventful, smooth, and comfortable; and Hans did not expect anything to change. The CIA had probably figured out that he was in Columbia; they had all kinds of resources to discover his location. But his escape aboard a charter flight was unknown; at least, he thought so. And anyone that did know would only run into trouble when they decided to engage in a chase. Bormann had organized a small Nazi team at the airport to report to him if any potential CIA or other party started to ask questions about his departure. They were also tasked to ensure whoever was asking questions would develop mechanical problems with their own aircraft.

Getting confirmation from his team as he flew away from Columbia confirmed his suspicions; he was being followed, and they were not far behind. This would not be true much longer; he had made sure of that before leaving.

Chapter 4 Rough Weather

President Mitchell was sitting in the Oval Office reading the daily Intel report which was provided every morning. He always read the report and wrote notes in the margins, and then he questioned his staff on areas for which he wanted more information.

"Tony, what's on the schedule today? I know we have a staff meeting after lunch, what else do we have?" Mitchell asked his National Security Advisor, Tony Sanford.

"Darrell, the schedule is pretty light today; just the lunch meeting and then you have a visit by the Smithsonian Museum Director. He wants to discuss the new exhibit dedicated to those lost."

"Good, I need a little time to collect myself. I have been a little down lately, as you well know. Why not get a six pack and kick back this afternoon," Mitchell said smiling.

"You're serious?"

"Very serious, Tony, very."

"Okay, after the director, I will get some brews up here and we will kick back for a couple of hours."

"Where is the VP?" Mitchell asked.

"He is flying back from Florida this afternoon. Want me to get him in here as soon as he lands?"

"Yeah, I need him here as soon as he lands."

"Sir, are you feeling okay?" Sanford asked being very concerned.

"No I am not doing fine," Mitchell said slurring his words. He attempted to slam his hand down on his desk, but did not have the power or strength to make an impact.

"Whoa, sir, take it easy, calm down, I'll call the doctor," Sanford said as he tried to calm down Mitchell.

President Mitchell laid his head down on his desk and started to cry uncontrollably. Just then the door to the Oval Office opened and his personal secretary started to walk in.

"Ms. Johnson, not now, please," Sanford said to her; and she turned around and immediately walked back out and closed the door. She had the good sense to not repeat what she saw to anyone, ever. Once outside, she turned to the visitor standing at her desk and said, "Sorry, but the President is busy at the moment; can you come back later Mr. Soto?"

"Do you believe he will be long? I really need to discuss a very important matter with him as soon as possible," Mr. Soto,

South Korean Ambassador asked; he was sweating and seemed to be very nervous.

"Give me your contact number; and as soon as he is available, I will call you to come right over. But from the looks of the meeting going on in there, it will be a while," Mrs. Johnson said and walked around behind her desk.

"Okay, I was hoping he could see me now; this is very important," Mr. Soto said and handed her his business card which listed his cell phone number.

Meanwhile, inside the office, President Mitchell continued to cry. Tony Sanford picked up the phone on the President's desk and dialed the private number for Dr. Morganson, the White House Doctor.

"Hello, Doctor, this is Tony Sanford," he said after the phone was answered on the third ring. "Would you come up to the Oval Office quickly, use the back entrance."

"Is there a problem?"

"Possibly," Sanford said and then hung up the phone.

Ten minutes later, Doctor Morganson was examining President Mitchell. Getting him to calm down enough to lie on the sofa had not been easy. After checking his vital signs, he reached into his back and extracted a vial and syringe.

"Sir, I am going to give you a sedative and want you to rest," Morganson said as he prepared to administer the shot. "Mr. Sanford, I suggest that he cancel any meetings for the day and possibly for tomorrow too. We really need to get him over to Walter Reed for a complete exam." He administered the shot and then stood. After walking away from the President, he waved Sanford over and quietly spoke again, "He is suffering from a nervous breakdown, most likely stress induced. His blood pressure is way off the scale, and it is amazing he didn't have a stroke. Or quite possibly he did. Did he loose his balance or was his speech slurred? As I said, I need to do a complete exam, so let's move him to the hospital."

"He started to slur his speech. I will alert the VP and Secret Service as well as call for the helo. You stay with him, I will be right back."

Twenty minutes later, the president, Sanford, the doctor, and three secret service agents were walking out to the helo pad for the waiting helo. They would be at the hospital in fifteen minutes after taking off. The VP stepped into the Oval Office just as they were about to leave, got a quick briefing and then walked behind the desk he would occupy for the unforeseeable future. He was not briefed on **Operation Sundance** which involved Davin, Josh and operators from covert operations. That operation was on a need to know basis and he did not need to know at this point.

Chapter 5 Rally the Troops

Deep in the forest surrounding Berlin, there were many secret facilities; some used by the government for research and development; others used by clandestine organizations to hold secret meetings, hide illegal contraband or just hide. Gregory Dietrich had several locations around Germany, some located in what was once East Germany and others in the western part of the country. Gregory was at one of his secret facilities standing in the wings of a great auditorium where hundreds of his followers were waiting for him to speak. He was dressed as SS-Oberst-Gruppenfuhrer und Generaloberst der Waffen-SS (SS-Supreme group leader and colonel general of the Waffen-SS). Everyone in the auditorium was also dressed in the appropriate uniform of a Nazi Schutzstaffel 'SS' officer or enlisted person. "Sieg heil!" Gregory yelled when he walked out on the platform and in return his followers yelled "Sieg heil!" meaning Heil Victory! After repeating the Sieg heil and the salute, Gregory started into his speech.

"Our quest is about to end. We have reached a point in our attacks to bring this to a close and take our rightful place in the world, as its leaders!" A roar from the crowd went up and another Sieg heil.

"We have come a long way and the end is near. Are the cameras on?" After getting a nod from the operator, he continued, "We are transmitting to all our followers around the world. They, like you, are committed to the completion of our mission, a mission that was started many years ago by our grandfathers. Our fathers, grandfathers, and brothers have died in this quest, but we will prevail. The last phase of our quest is about to begin. They will do their part and you will do yours. You have been issued your weapons, trained for this, and are ready to conquer the world. We will not fail! Now let us begin. At midnight tonight, America will feel our power and bow down to us. Sieg heil!" Gregory concluded with his raised right arm in the Nazi salute.

At the same time Gregory was giving his followers their final pep talk, his sister Michelle was boarding a plane heading for Los Angeles, California. Her dream of becoming a Hollywood star was soon to be realized, at least so she thought. Unknown to her was the biological bomb she was carrying within her body. Of course, her brother did not want her to die, so she was a carrier only. An antidote had been administered to her prior to departure. She had no idea about what she carried or the extent of the damage it would cause.

Four hours before her flight, while eating breakfast with her brother, the antidote was fed to her in her eggs and the virus was passed to her via her orange juice. Although feeling a little nervous about the flight, she was happy about getting the chance to prove herself to the world as a super star; she was ready to leave her home country for a new life.

Her brother, whom she loved dearly, had contacted an old friend that was in the movie business and set up an interview and screen test. She was excited and scared at the same time. She had been told to take a cab to the Hollywood Hilton and the next morning call and meet with the producer.

Upon boarding her flight, she took her seat in first class, took the glass of white wine from the steward, and leaned back for the long flight, smiling. She was happy and sad, happy to be going to America but sad for leaving her brother and country. She had dressed conservatively in a pair of jeans and long sleeve grey blouse and boots. She loved boots, especially tall ones with heels.

A young man sat in the seat beside her and introduced himself as Jackson Mendelson, a movie producer, writer and director. Their conversation quickly turned to making movies and she asked, "How can I get into one of your movies?"

"We can do a screen test next week if you like. Where are you staying?"

"Hollywood Hilton."

"Good, just down the street from my studio," Jackson replied.

The flight to America was smooth and full of plans between the two first class passengers. As they spoke, her virus was incubating and starting to infect everyone on the plane. By the time they reached New York all three hundred and twenty passengers and crew would be very sick. The virus was spreading faster than predicted by Dietrich and his medical team.

Chapter 6 The Korean Connection

"Hello, this is Mi-Cha Sang," Agent Joanne Morgan said into her phone after the second ring; hopefully, this was the call she was waiting for. She was watching the people of her country of birth walk by. Unknown to them, she was a field operative working for the CIA on an undercover mission to locate and arrest the individual that ordered the launch of eight nuclear ICBMs at the United States. They were completely unaware of this incident that had almost caused their country to go into another war, a war they would have had no way of winning. She was in the small town of Kaesong, North Korea, just north of the border. She would enter South Korea in a few minutes and head for Seoul to catch a flight to France. If all went well, she would be sipping wine in southern France by morning.

"Ms Sang, this is Fred Hirshman," Hirshman said and then automatically switched to secure transmission. Sang also pressed a button on the side of her cell phone which switched her phone to secure mode also. "The individual you are looking for is retired General Jin-Ho Shin. He is staying in a villa in the town of Marseille on the coast in the south of France."

"Yes, that is him; I have confirmed he is missing and presumed to be a defector, along with a Doctor Jang and a woman. Fred, where are you now?"

"We are in Marseille staying at the Sofitel Marseille Vieux-Port. Want me to book you a room?" Fred asked. "I cannot confirm the whereabouts of Doctor Jang, but the General has a woman with him. Not sure who she is, but will work on it."

"Yes, I will be there as soon as tomorrow, if I can get a flight out," Sang replied and then paused for a moment before continuing, "No, find me a villa or hotel close to our target. Are you keeping a close eye on him?"

"Yes, my partner is watching the villa this morning; I will take over in a couple of hours."

"Good, I will be there as quickly as possible," Sang commented and then broke the connection.

She sat outside a small coffee shop enjoying the sunshine, sipping her latte, and thinking about her upcoming trip. She saw them coming, three men in black suits, walking slowing up the street. The hairs on the back of her neck started to stand; something was wrong. She wasn't sure what or why, but Joanne had a bad feeling about what she saw. At the same time, coming from the opposite direction, were three police officers or what were considered the police in North Korea. They were dressed in military uniforms and carrying automatic weapons; none of them smiled. The three she was looking at stopped at her table and in near perfect English spoke.

"Mi-Cha Sang?" the lead man asked looking deep into her eyes.

"Yes, how may I help you?" she asked in perfect Korean, not breaking eye contact.

"You will come with us, now," he stated in English not reverting to his native language.

"Am I being arrested for drinking coffee on a beautiful morning?" Sang asked in Korean again.

"Please, we do not want to cause an incident, Ms Sang!"

"May I finish my latte?"

"Yes you may," he said as he sat in the chair across from her and indicated for his two men to take a seat also. Then he looked down the street at the armed military men and smiled. They had stopped a half block away and stood eying Ms Sang and her visitors. One of the military reached over and spoke into his radio as he kept his eyes on Ms Sang and her visitors.

"Would you care for a latte, Mister?" she asked.

"No thank you Ms Sang. We do need to get going; can you drink a little faster before our friends down the street get too antsy," he responded but did not introduce himself. "Don't bother to look down the street. They are here to arrest you; we are here to make sure that does not happen. And who we are does not matter; what matters is that you are safe and able to cross the border today."

"Okay, I understand. I am finished, shall we go?" she said as she set her empty cup down and stood. The four of them turned and walked down the street to waiting cars and two more men and one woman; all were dressed in black suits. Their weapons were obvious in shoulder holsters and all looked very capable in handling most situations. Sang was very observant; but, at first glance, she did not see any weapon larger than a pistol.

Chapter 7 Columbia

"You know, Butch, we could be home with a cold beer, watching the tele with our wives; but, no, we are down here looking for someone that wants both of us dead. Why don't we just let him come to us, on our own turf?" Davin, aka, Sundance, said to his partner as they drove on a narrow winding road heading for a villa located outside of town where Hans Bormann was last seen. Behind them were two more vehicles carrying the rest of their team, fifteen Columbia Special Weapons squad and two more CIA agents.

"Yes, but when he shows up, he usually brings a whole bunch of trouble. It is best we take him down before he can organize his team and cause the country problems," Josh, aka, Butch responded. "Look, we are almost there." He pulled over to the side of the road and turned off the engine. "The villa is just around the bend; we should walk from here."

"It's got to be one hundred degrees out there," Davin protested. Even with the air conditioner running at maximum, they were both sweating.

"Yeah, quit complaining; let's just get this guy and go home."

"Okay, okay," Davin agreed; he pulled his Colt 45 out of its shoulder holster and checked that he had a round in the chamber and a full magazine. Josh did the same with his weapon and then slid out of the driver's seat and walked back to the first truck. "The villa is just ahead; take your men and secure the area. Make sure no one gets out of that compound. But don't kill anyone! Understand? Just detain them."

"Yes, sir," the sergeant responded and then jumped out to organize his men. Josh then returned to his car and addressed Agents Rafael Jordan and Season Garcia. "Okay, guys, here's the deal. Your informant placed Bormann in the villa ahead. Correct?"

"Yes, we have not verified this ourselves, but she is a reliable source. This is the home of Juan Ortiz, a suspected drug dealer; and she has been working there for about a year. She has kept us, and the local cops, informed on everything that she can. As I said back at the base, as of this morning, he was here."

"Let's get going; it is only getting hotter," Josh said and they all started to walk toward the villa. With the army surrounding the villa, Josh, Davin, Rafael and Season approached from the front. They casually walked down the sidewalk toward the door.

"What's the plan?" Rafael asked as they approached the front door. Nobody had pulled their weapons as they stepped onto the porch.

"Knock on the door and see what it brings," Josh replied and immediately knocked on the door, turned and looked at his three friends, smiling.

"May I help you?" a voice asked as the door opened.

"Yes, we are here to see Hans Bormann; we understand he is staying here," Josh said to the older gentlemen who answered the door.

"There is no Hans Bormann here," the gentlemen replied smiling.

"Sure there is; he called me just awhile ago asking for us to stop by," Josh lied.

"Mr. Bormann is not here, sir. You may come in and look for yourself if you like, but he left two hours ago," the gentleman said as he opened the door to let the four agents enter the house. They split up to search the house and within minutes they had covered the entire home and only found two young ladies dressed in tiny string bikinis laying by the pool. They also said that Bormann had left a couple of hours earlier.

They walked back to the car and gathered up the military; they headed back toward the base feeling at a loss for not finding Bormann.

"Now what?" Season asked.

"You and Rafael check with the airport and see if he was on any of the scheduled airlines; and Davin and I will check on any charter flights. Make sure you look at the video camera footage, and, well, you know the routine. Meet back at baggage claim in two hours. We will send the Army back to their base."

"Okay, drop us off at departures and we will call if we have anything."

Chapter 8 Escape from North Korea

Mi-Cha Sang climbed into the waiting sedan and strapped on her seat belt. The driver started the engine and pulled away from the curb just as sirens could be heard approaching.

"Move it, Max!" the lead man in black said to the driver. "We have company coming."

"Roger that!" the driver replied and then accelerated away from the curb with the second car close behind. "Heading for the border; think they will stop us at the border."

"Yep! They will most certainly try to stop us. Keep it at the speed limit, at least for now," he ordered.

"Who are you guys?" Sang asked becoming very concerned.

"We are the 'A' Team, anyway that is what they call us back at Langley. Our only mission in life is search and recovery. Whenever an agent goes deep cover, we are deployed to provide backup and rescue if need be. We were put together to go in and locate potential agents in distress and get them out of the mess they are in. You, Ms Sang, turned over a few rocks that got the attention of some very nasty people. People that want to keep certain things quiet. The General you were looking for still has friends here to cover his butt, and they pulled some strings and now have the military out looking for you. And when they find you, well, you will end up in a dark hole somewhere, never to be seen again. Although the north and south have decided to rejoin, they still have a small border crossing facility. Should not be a problem sliding by. Catch my drift?"

"Yes, I do; I am usually very quiet about what I do. I guess I turned one rock too many," Sang stated.

"Here they come, sir!"

"We are eighteen miles from the border, step on it," he ordered just as a burst of automatic rifle fire hit the back of the trailing vehicle.

"Taking fire back here; let's move it," the rear vehicle passenger yelled into the radio and then reached down and picked up an M-4 rifle, a modified compact M-16 with collapsible stock and short barrel. He dropped the safety and turned in his seat to get ready to return fire when given permission to do so.

"Hold fire, we don't want an international incident, do we?" Another burst of rifle fire slammed into the rear vehicle.

"They are closing the gap, sir!" the second vehicle radioed ahead.

"We have another problem, stay close," the lead agent stated, pointing ahead at the two military vehicles blocking the road. The driver made a hard right hand turn to avoid the road block. The ride got faster and more dangerous as they proceeded; once they left the city and were running at nearly eighty miles per hour, the shooting got a bit heavier from the chase vehicles.

"Return fire, but be careful of your target," the lead ordered and almost immediately, he heard the unmistakable sound of an M-4 rifle. The road was windy and had a lot of dips which caused the cars to leave the ground and go airborne almost as much as they were on the ground. The constant bullet strikes on the rear vehicles rear window finally caused the bullet proof glass to lose strength and crack. The agent in the back seat used the hole in the rear window to his advantage. He placed the barrel of his weapon out the hole and fired directly at the vehicle behind them. Bullets rained down on both vehicles punching holes in each of them.

The race to the border did not last long; the military had a lot of help and cut off several possible routes with blockades. Eighteen miles went pretty quick for the 'A' Team, but not quick enough. They crossed the border without a problem, but the military continued to follow. They fired constantly and eventually shot out one of the rear tires of the second sedan. It spun off the road and ended up in a ditch; all three occupants were injured but survived the crash. The military did not stop to check on them or arrest anyone. They continued on bearing down on the lone sedan with Ms Sang clutching tightly to the dashboard.

"They are still coming!" she yelled.

"Not for long," the lead agent replied and raised his hand to his ear and clicked the Bluetooth. "Henry, you guys okay back there?"

"Yeah, a little banged up, but okay; they did not even stop," Henry replied over the radio.

"We will be back to get you soon."

"Roger that, sir. We will be fine."

"They are slowing down, sir," the driver noticed in his rear view mirror. "Yep, slowing down."

"Oh, hell, they have an RPG," the driver said again as he watched in his mirror. "They are firing!" he yelled and then turned the sedan hard to the left to keep from being hit by the shell. It exploded not more than fifty feet from them; the car received a lot of the shrapnel but was able to continue. "Firing again!"

He turned again to the left, hoping to fool the gunner, which he did. But it might not work again; he pushed down on the pedal, causing the car to leap to over one hundred miles per hour, hoping he could outrun the gun's range.

"I've had enough of this," Sang yelled, "Stop the car, now!"

"What?" the driver yelled.

"STOP THE DAMN CAR!" she yelled again.

The driver slammed on the brakes and skidded to a stop, sliding sideways and stopping in the middle of the road. Sang jumped from the car and pulled a large automatic pistol from her bag. The chasing military vehicles continued toward them stopping about seventy feet away. The door to the front car opened and out stepped a tall female Korean officer. She raised her hand indicating she wanted her men to stop shooting, which they did immediately but did not lower their weapons. She started to walk toward Sang and her rescuers stopping about twenty-five feet from her. And in perfect English she spoke.

"Mi-Cha Sang, I need you to come with me," she stated.

"Are you arresting me?"

"No, we have some questions for you."

"Ask your questions, I am not going back," she yelled still holding her automatic pistol, trigger finger resting on the trigger guard. "Turn your vehicles around and go back north before the army gets here. They are on the way."

"Another time, Sang, another time," she yelled back, walked back to the car, climbed in and headed back north. Sang and her rescuers got back into their car and headed to Seoul. They checked with Henry. The army had arrived at the crash site and the occupants of the crashed vehicle were being transported to Seoul. "Who was that woman?" Sang asked the leader of her rescuers.

"That was General Soon-Bok Kim; she is in charge of the Secret Police for all of North Korea, not someone to screw with." "She obviously knows who I am and I guess my cover in North Korea is blown."

"Yep!"

Chapter 9 Can We Get Frequent Flyer Miles?

"Where to sir?" the pilot of the CIA Corporate jet asked as Davin and Josh boarded the plane. They were followed by Rafael and Season. After canvassing the commercial and general aviation terminals for the past three hours, they were all disgusted and tired.

"Grab a seat guys; we need to talk," Josh offered and then turned to the pilot sitting in the cockpit. "No where just yet; what is the range of this bird?"

"Depends, at normal cruise, we can make it to the coast of Africa, Bermuda, almost anywhere in the southern U.S. with a full load of fuel."

"Good, get us full; we may be leaving shortly, and I don't know where we are going yet," Josh ordered.

"I will check and see if the military can fuel us; if not, we may have to taxi over to general aviation."

"Make it happen," Josh ordered and then turned to the steward, a cute young woman with a smile that could melt a man's heart. But today, he just needed a drink. "Mandy, do we have any cold beer on board?"

"Yes, Coors, Miller, Bud, Heineken, and I think we have a couple Alaskan Amber. And my name is Mary," Mary replied.

"Sorry Mary, would you bring me the Amber and see what everyone else wants. Bring some snacks too; we have some planning to do," he said and then headed into the cabin with Davin, Season, and Rafael.

"Okay boys and girl, what have we got?" Josh asked as he entered the cabin.

"Well, Season and I checked every flight, the manifests, video files and destinations on every flight that left within the past five hours. And, well, we were able to narrow it down to four flights that had a possible Bormann on board. Destinations included LA, Miami, Havana and Monrovia in western Africa."

"No other possible?"

"No, actually those are the only flights that departed in the last five hours. Not a very busy airport," Season replied.

"Okay, we were a little bit luckier, I guess; there were only two charter flights and several smaller aircraft departing from here in the past few hours. There were three small aircraft departing; two returned, and they were just returning from an hour of time-building, working toward their commercial ratings. The third has not returned yet and the flight plan says one pilot and one passenger, only the pilot's name was listed; destination, Panama City, Panama. The plane is a twin engine Piper Navajo."

"So what's the plan, Butch?" Davin piped in.

"I want more information on that Piper, before we go flying off all over the place," Josh recommended, "Season, contact Harold Jenkins at the FAA and see if he can get more information on that Panama flight."

"On it," she replied and then stood and walked over to a computer terminal and looked up the cell phone number for Harold Jenkins.

"Rafael, follow up on those commercial flights. He left Bogota today; he can't be that hard to track. Davin and I are going to Panama. Haven't been there for awhile, would be good to see the changes."

"Harold said he will call you as soon as he has anything on the Panama flight," Season reported a few minutes later.

"We have to taxi over to general aviation for fuel, Mr. Randal. They are unable to fuel us here," the pilot said as he stuck his head into the cabin. "As soon as you are ready, we can move."

"We will be ready in a moment," Josh commented and then turned to Season and Rafael, "Report back to me as soon as you have anything."

Chapter 10 Seoul, Korea

"Mr. Hancock, please," Mi-Cha Sang asked over her secure satellite phone.

"Stand by, Ms Sang," the voice on the other end said without emotion.

"Ms Sang we need you to come home. Abort the mission and return home," a female voice finally said after a long three minute wait.

"Why, what has happened?" she asked.

"Mr. Hancock, your controller was found dead yesterday in his hotel room. Your cover is blown." After a short pause, he continued, "The 'A' Team will help you get out of the country."

"Who is this? Can I speak with Mr. Randal?" Sang asked.

"Mr. Randal and Mr. Pierce are out of the country. You need to return," the female voice repeated.

"Who is this?"

"This is Ashley Peterson, Director CIA. Report to me directly when you get home and only to me, understand, Ms Morgan," Peterson said and the line went dead.

Joanne Morgan looked over at the team leader and smiled, "I guess I am going home, now."

"Yep. I don't know what happened, but I do know that your life is in danger the longer you stay in country. We have a plane waiting at the airport that will get us back to Washington."

"What happens to your team?"

"We have been compromised too. The rest of the team will meet us at the airport and we all fly out, today," he said and then turned and walked back to his car. "Let's go; we are burning daylight."

"As you command, my lord," Sang said smiling and then walked back to the car, putting her satellite phone back into her pack beside her Glock Model 30 automatic pistol.

An hour and half later, Joanne and the team were boarding a Boeing 747, not your ordinary 747, this one was a flying command center, similar to one the President flew in, known as Air Force One. The biggest difference was this one was painted as a United Airlines jet. United provided regular service to Korea, Japan, China and most of the Pacific islands, so seeing it on the ramp parked at a United Airlines terminal gate was not anything that would draw attention. The only thing that would have attracted attention was when several Chevy Tahoes pulled up beside the plane, and passengers and bags were unloaded directly into the plane, not passing through normal security checks.

Minutes after the fifteen men and one woman boarded the plane, the doors were closed. The pilot had the ground crew push the big airplane back and allow it to taxi to the active runway for an immediate departure, by-passing several other aircraft waiting to depart.

After leveling off at thirty-five thousand feet, the pilot unbuckled and tapped his co-pilot on the shoulder and quietly said, "You have the bird, Amy." The pilot headed back to the cabin passing though the communications bay located on the second deck and then down the spiral stairs to the main cabin.

"Good afternoon lady and gentlemen; welcome to United CIA Flight seventy-two, bound for Washington D.C. I am Colonel Nick Brady; I came down from the flight deck to welcome you on your flight home. I apologize for the quick departure, but my orders are to get you back home safely and as quickly as possible. I don't know why, so don't ask. My crew, consisting of Amy Johnson, copilot, Jane, Kate, Fred and John, are your cabin crew and then we have several more up in the communications center. I have to ask each of you not to come upstairs for any reason. Your clearance level does not allow it;

but if you need to call anyone, please ask one of the cabin crew to show you the communication room on this deck. There is an armed guard at the top of the stairs to remind you not to come up. Sorry about that, but I don't make the rules, just enforce them," Brady said and then took a moment to look around the well appointed main cabin; it was set up more as an executive jet instead of a passenger liner.

"Colonel, do you serve food on this luxury liner?" the lead of the team asked.

"Yes, they will be serving drinks and dinner shortly; we just need to get out of Korean airspace before they send out fighters to turn us back."

"Colonel" the overhead speaker spoke.

"Yes, Amy," Brady responded on the closest microphone.

"We have company."

"Please excuse me, those are the bad guys I mentioned; we are still in Korean airspace for the next ten minutes anyway, and they may want us to turn around. I'll be back," Colonel Brady said and then turned and headed for the cockpit.

"Wow. That was heavy," Joanne Morgan said to the leader of the team.

"Yeah, makes you wonder what this plane really does?" he commented.

"Me too."

"Attention everyone, all is well, the company we have are US Air Force F-35s out of Alaska; they have been sent to escort us until we are well away from Korea. Cabin crew you may start drink and dinner service. Enjoy," Colonel Brady said over the aircraft intercom to everyone on board.

Chapter 11 Panama City, Panama

After a short flight from Bogotá, Davin and Josh landed in Panama City, Panama. After stepping out the door into the sunshine, they looked intently at each other and thought, *'Just as hot as ever.'*

"Josh did you ever get a tour down here?" Davin asked as he looked around the airport.

"Yeah, spent almost a year here before I was shipped to Nam. The field station was located about ten miles in the jungle off of Fort Clayton."

"I remember that place; turned over to another government agency supposedly. A friend took me out there to show me where it was, but we never got inside. I got here long after you; remember, we met in Nam, and when my tour was up, they sent me here," Davin replied thinking back to those days. "Where do you want to start? Maybe find the owner of that Navajo over there" he said pointing to a Piper Navajo twin engine plane sitting on the tarmac about two hundred feet from where they had parked.

"Mr. Randal, should we wait at the plane or get a room?" the copilot asked.

"Get her fueled and ready; I will call shortly to tell you, but wait here until," Josh answered and started to walk down the stairs.

Within minutes, they were walking around the Navajo. Davin turned and headed for the terminal with hopes of locating the pilot in the café or somewhere in the building. Josh turned and followed close behind.

Once inside the building, Davin headed for the café; and Josh turned and walked over to the flight planning room in the Fixed Base Operations Center.

"Hello, can you tell me where I can find the pilot to that Navajo?" Josh asked the attendant behind the desk.

"He came in and filed a flight plan for a flight to Bogotá, Columbia with a departure of, let's see, oh here it is, he is planning on flying out in the morning at 9 am."

"Thank you; do you know where he is now? I would like to charter his plane," Josh explained as he continued his questioning.

"Yes, he called for a cab and went to a hotel. I believe he said the Hilton Panama."

"Thank you. Oh, what does he look like?" Josh said just as Davin walked up behind him.

"Six foot, black hair, streaks of grey, a little overweight, probably two hundred fifty pounds, around forty years of age, graying at the temples, wearing jeans and a white shirt," the attendant said, with a questionable look on his face.

"Thank you; hopefully, we can find him," Josh said and then turned to Davin.

"What did you find out?" Davin asked. "He is not in the café."

"Plenty, let's go."

As they walked outside, they scanned over the airport, drawing up memories of days gone by, the good times and bad, by being in the Army.

"Let's go back to the plane and let the crew know what is going on and book a hotel," Josh said as they walked back toward the jet. "Okay, let's say Bormann got on that Navajo and flew here and then chartered another plane or just got on a commercial jet and flew somewhere. Where do you think he is going?"

"He is German; I would assume he is heading back home."

"That is a good assumption, Sundance; but what if he has a different agenda? What if he is going back to the United States to follow through with his threat? Let's say he is going back to D.C. with a plan. Where does that leave us? We are thousands of miles away with no more information than we had two days ago."

"Yeah, he could be heading for D.C. or almost anywhere else on this pretty big world of ours; but I promise you one thing old friend, we will catch him and we will, or rather I will, put a hole in his head before he can cause any more damage."

"Not if I see him first," Josh replied.

"I get to shoot him first, Butch; he almost killed me, and he kidnapped my wife."

"Well, hell, that does give you a shot; but he almost killed my best friend and kidnapped his wife, so that gives me first right to shoot."

"How do you figure that? Look, we both shoot together; he dies as soon as we see him," Davin replied.

"Deal, but let's try to get some information from him before we kill him," Josh requested.

"Okay, a little information and a lot of bullets," Davin stated as they started to climb the stairs to the corporate jet.

"Captain, call the Hilton Panama and book us some rooms; we will be staying the night," Josh ordered the pilot as they entered the jet.

"Yes sir," the pilot acknowledged and then stepped back into the cockpit.

Morning came early for everyone. Having browsed all the bars around the hotel and a few more a short cab ride further the night before, the team didn't really appreciate awaking even though it was to a beautiful sunrise and hot coffee. The plan was to meet at 6:15 in the hotel restaurant for breakfast and then head out to the airport. They were hoping to catch the pilot of the Navajo before he took off. Breakfast was good and hot, and they departed the hotel at 7:30 for the ride to the airport arriving at 8:20 a.m.

As they exited the terminal, Davin and Josh saw a man walking around the Navajo. Their pilot and co-pilot went to flight planning to check the weather for a flight to somewhere unknown at the moment.

"There he is, Butch," Davin 'Sundance' said as they walked across the tarmac toward the Navajo.

"Good morning," Josh yelled as they approached.

"Good morning," a smiling man of about forty years old said in return. "What can I do for you on this beautiful morning?"

"You just flew in yesterday with a passenger?" Davin asked.

"Yes, nice fellow paid in cash. Paid well too, twice what I normally charge for a short flight," he replied.

"Did he look like this man?" Josh asked and handed him a picture of Hans Bormann.

"Yes, is he in trouble or something? Am I in trouble for flying him here? If I had known, I wouldn't have flown him here; but he said he had business in town, and then he was catching a flight to Bermuda to meet his girl friend."

"No, you are not in trouble; but he is," Davin stated and then asked, "Are you sure he flew to Bermuda?"

"That's what he said. He grabbed a cab and left pretty quickly," the pilot said.

"Any idea of the name of the cab company?" Josh asked.

"No, I was closing up the bird; and once he paid me, I didn't really care where he went," the pilot said and then added, "Now I have to finish my preflight and get back to Bogotá for another charter; will you excuse me?"

"Sure, thanks for the information," Davin finished and they walked toward their own plane.

"What now, Butch?"

"He had business in town and then off to Bermuda, on a commercial flight or charter? Let's check charter first. He does not fly commercial because of the security and he may be identified and detained. Back to the terminal," Josh said and then turned and trotted to the terminal and walked into the flight planning area looking for the attendant. He found him leaning over an aeronautical chart of Panama.

"Hello again. Can you tell me if there were any charter flights leaving yesterday afternoon?" Josh asked.

"Sure, why?" the attendant asked becoming very annoyed with Josh.

"I asked if there were any charter flights departing here yesterday afternoon?" Josh repeated himself.

"Okay, don't get so snippety. We had one Legacy 650 depart here with one passenger, crew of three on an international flight to Bermuda. Distance of one thousand six hundred eighty-five nautical miles or one thousand nine hundred thirty-nine air miles, well within their range of about thirty-nine hundred nautical miles for that bird."

"Thanks," Josh said to the attendant and then turned to his pilot and said, "Guess we are off to Bermuda."

Chapter 12 Washington D.C.

"Mr. Sanford, our president has suffered from a small stroke. It could have killed him, but lucky for him and us it didn't. I have to keep him here a few days for observation. Is the VP back in town?" the president's doctor reported to Sanford later that day.

"Damn, yes, the VP is back in town," Sanford replied and thinking he continued, "We will report that the president is in for his annual checkup. That will keep the press hounds from bearing down on us."

"There is something else you need to know."

"What is it?"

"I am not sure yet, but it looks like he has been poisoned. Now we don't have positive proof; however, the preliminary tox screen showed traces of a poison that is slow in reacting, but deadly. Once we narrow it down, we should be able to eradicate it."

"Poisoned, how, when?"

"That is a good question my young friend. It may have happened when he was a captive in Iran. That is the most likely place."

"Keep me posted on his condition and the poison. I need to get back to the White House and inform the VP," Sanford said and then turned to leave.

"Mr. Sanford, also tell the VP that I will be here for the next few days. My nurse is on call if he needs anything medical." Sanford left the hospital and headed back to the White House. While driving, after a brief stop at a coffee shop on the way back, he got the feeling he was being followed. After looking in his rear view mirrors, he was able to confirm that a black van had been following him since he left the hospital. Thinking to himself, he wondered, *'Now who the hell is that back there?'*

As he turned into the White House entry, he stopped at the White House gate and informed the guard to watch the black van that was passing by while he continued to talk to the guard. The guard was able to get the license plate number as it passed; after writing it on a 3x5 card, he handed it to Sanford.

"Thank you, Sergeant," Sanford said as he took the card from the guard, "I will get metro to check it out."

Minutes later, Sanford was walking into the Oval Office to see the Vice President. After informing the VP on the condition of the president, he turned and left. He went back to his office to contact the Staff Duty Officer of the Secret Service on duty.

"Hello Mr. Polson, how are you doing on this wonderful day?"

"As well as can be expected; all is quiet today. What can I do for you, Mr. Sanford?" Polson asked.

"Can you come over to my office, I have something to discuss with you," Sanford requested.

"Be there in a couple of minutes," Polson responded and quickly turned and headed toward Sanford's office.

"A black van tailed me from the hospital, kind of suspicious, but most likely just a reporter looking for a quick story," Sanford said as soon as Polson entered his office and then handed Polson a card with the license plate number written on it. "Don't do anything yet; let's find out who it is first. Report back to me as soon as you get the owner's name."

"No problem sir," Polson acknowledged and then left Sanford's office, walking briskly down the hall toward the Secret Service office.

'What the hell else could happen today?' Sanford said to himself just as his phone started to ring. "Sanford."

"Peterson, are you busy, we need to talk," Ashley Peterson, Director CIA asked.

"Yes, but it sounds urgent. Come on over," Sanford responded, "Or is it something we can talk about over the phone?"

"No, see you in twenty minutes, I am almost there," she said and the line clicked off.

Fifteen minutes later, Ashley Peterson was walking down the hall toward Sanford's office with a very concerned look on her face. She entered the outer office and approached the desk of his secretary who immediately looked up and then pointed toward the door to Sanford's office. "The door's open; go on in, he's waiting."

"Thank you," Ashley said and then entered Sanford's office and sat in a chair directly across from Sanford's desk.

"What has gotten you so riled?" Sanford asked seeing the concern on her face.

"We have a serious problem, Tony," Ashley started, "One of my top deep agents recently had her cover compromised. But that is not the problem. We will recover from that. However, before she was compromised, she was able to acquire information indicating a connection between the individual that launched the ICBMs at us and a high level Nazi organizer."

"A Nazi organizer, what the hell is going on? This is 2015, the Nazis are all dead and buried. Aren't they?" Sanford responded shaking his head in disbelief.

Chapter 13 Bermuda

The flight from Panama was uneventful; Davin slept most of the way while Josh made several phone calls. He attempted to speak to the President, but was told he was not available.

"We are on approach into Bermuda, please fasten your seat belts and prep the cabin for landing," the copilot announced over the cabin intercom.

"Davin wake up, we are landing," Josh said as he shook his partner. "Fasten your seat belt."

"Oh, okay, where are we?"

"Landing in Bermuda."

"Okay, what took us so long?" Davin said through the fog.

"We have some information on the person who launched the ICBMs at us."

"Good, fill me in after a cup of coffee." After pausing for a moment, he looked over at the steward and asked, "Could I get a cup of black coffee, PLEASE?"

"As soon as we land, I will bring you a cup of coffee, Mr. Pierce," she replied.

"Thank you, Jane."

"My name is Mary, not Jane, sir. Would you like that coffee in a cup or prefer to wear it?" she replied with a sneaky smile.

"Sorry… Cup, please, Mary."

The landing was as smooth as if they were still flying; only a small chirp of the tires touching the pavement was heard. They taxied to the general aviation terminal and shut down. Davin got his cup of coffee and then turned to face Josh.

"Have you ever been here, Davin?" Josh asked and looked out the window.

"Yes, Connie and I came here a while back for a quick weekend away. Beautiful island, great food and as they say, if you didn't bring it here, you may not find it here; it's an island. Unless you are born here or grow it here, it has to be brought in by air or boat," Davin answered.

"Okay, we need to find that charter jet that should have arrived a few hours ago. Then we decide what to do next. Let's go," Josh said and then stood up and started for the door. He stopped short when his secure satellite phone rang. *'Oh hell, now what?'* he thought

"Butch and Sundance Pizza, how can I help you?" Josh said into the phone, which had immediately gone to secure when he pushed the answer button.

"Three large pepperoni pizzas and two large Coors, to go," Ashley Peterson responded with the appropriate answer. It was a check and balance system. First the system went to secure mode, but to ensure that the parties that were speaking were the ones you wanted to speak with, they had a code worked out, sign and countersign. And the improper answer would alert the other that they were not who they were supposed to be.

"Yes, Ashley. What can the Wild Bunch do for you on this beautiful afternoon?" Josh asked.

"It is not what you can do for me, but what I can do for you. We have received information from a reliable source that Hans Bormann is connected to a very sophisticated, highly motivated, and financed Nazi organization. We now know who launched the ICBMs and are in the process of picking him up and then we will know more. But be warned, they are large and strong with a lot of connections around the world. You also need to know that the president is in the hospital; he had a stroke. We are keeping that under wraps for now; only Sanford, the hospital staff, me, and now you, know he is there. The VP is running the country and he does not know about your mission. I am not going to brief him just yet. And that Legacy 650 you have been looking for left Bermuda four hours ago, destination Madrid, Spain."

"Damn, a day late and a dollar short. Anything else you want to dump on us?" Josh asked. "I am going to brief Davin on what you said; he needs to know."

"Sure, safe trip," Ashley said and then ended the call.

"Captain, get us refueled and file for Madrid. We leave as soon as you are ready," Josh ordered the pilot and then looked at Davin. "Get yourself some more coffee, we leave as soon as we are fueled and they have the flight plan submitted."

"Madrid, but I wanted to bum around Bermuda for a while. Pick up a few trinkets," Davin said kidding his best friend and partner.

"Mary, do we need to stock more food?" Josh asked.

"Just some more beverages, but we do have enough to make the trip, if you don't want to drink much."

"We will not be drinking," Josh replied smiling, "Not on this leg."

Chapter 14 Marseille, France

Lieutenant Commander Dan Price surveyed the villa with his night vision binoculars. He saw no movement in or around it. Quietly he pressed the button on the headset mounted on his left ear and spoke in a whisper. "Blue team in position, no movement seen," he reported to Ashley Peterson via the satellite link they had established earlier.

"Roger, Blue One," Ashley replied from her operations center located in the basement of CIA Headquarters in Langley, Virginia. "Stand by."

"Standing by," Price responded and then double-clicked the headset to connect with his team. "We are on standby, prepare to move out."

They were Seal Team Six, world famous for taking down Osama Bin Laden. And, now, they were about to raid a villa in Marseille, France to capture, not kill, a North Korean General by the name of Jin-Ho Shin, a fugitive from North Korea, and accused of launching eight ICBMs at the United States in violation of his own government's wishes. He was considered rogue and a war criminal. They were to capture and bring him to the United States for trail.

"Blue One, execute, execute, execute," Peterson said three times to ensure the command was clear to Lt. Commander Price. Immediately, Price ordered his men to move; and with much practiced precision, they moved into the villa quietly and completely unseen by anyone, so they thought. Going through the villa only took three minutes and what they found was not what they expected. An elderly Korean male was lying face down in the hallway with two bullet holes in his back. He was later identified as Dr. Jang. Upon reaching the master suite, they found a nearly nude middle-aged woman, bound hand and foot, unconscious on the bed. She was identified as Mrs. Jang, her dead husband was downstairs. After quickly getting her dressed, they exited the villa and headed to the evac area located four miles outside the city. Mrs. Jang accompanied them. In broken English, she described what had happened.

"They came in fast. Dressed in black, like Ninja. Shoot my husband, forced me upstairs and tied me up. General Shin was not there when they came. I know not where they go. They fast," she said, trying her best not to cry.

"Thank you," Lt. Commander Price said to her and then reported what he found out to Ashley Peterson back at Langley.

"Blue One, put her on a plane with two of my people and send her here. Take your team and see if you can locate the attackers that got there first. Leave the place as you found it; do not call the local authorities. Relocate your team; we do not want the local authorities finding you there. Get me Shin," Peterson ordered.

"Understand, will have her on the plane in forty-five. My team is already working on locating the other team and General Shin. They beat us this time, but will not beat us again. Blue One, out," Price acknowledged and broke the connection.

Twenty-three minutes later, Price had turned Mrs. Jang over to two CIA operatives in a field outside of town; and they escorted her to a waiting helicopter which would fly them to the nearest international airport where a corporate jet was waiting to fly to the United States. She did not resist or say much of anything during the trip to the helicopter or to the airport. Upon reaching the airport, she attempted to escape twice, but was unsuccessful. Once on the jet, she calmed down; and after a few drinks, she became very talkative. She told the agents everything from receiving the money to actually firing the missiles. She did not understand why her husband and Shin wanted to destroy the United States, but she did understand the money. They took very good notes and also recorded the conversation as they flew across the Atlantic Ocean.

New York J.F. Kennedy International Airport

"New York approach control, American Airlines eight five four is with you at flight level three eight. We wish to declare an emergency," the pilot stated without waiting for approach control to respond.

"American eight five four, approach control, what is the nature of the emergency?"

"Approach, we may have a plane load of very sick people; almost every passenger his come down with fever, sweats and flu-like conditions, including my co-pilot and most of the crew. I am not well, and don't know how much longer I can control this plane. Flying on autopilot right now."

"American eight five four stand by."
"Don't be too long, approach," the pilot responded quietly and then filled another bag as he threw up again. The minutes passed but very slowly before the radio spoke again.

"American eight five four, can you land the plane?"

"Yes, we are on autopilot now and..." the pilot answered and then went silent.

"American eight five four, are you okay?" asked the supervisor in the approach control center.

"I am here..." the pilot came back in a very weak voice.

"Okay, we are clearing you to land immediately on runway three one left. We are clearing all traffic. Descend immediately and turn left when reaching five thousand. Make straight in approach to runway three one left. Stay on this frequency."

"Descending to five thousand out of...ahhh flight level three eight. Turn left at five thousand to three one zero. Make straight in to runway three one left."

"Once on the ground, pull off the runway and stop. We will have medical meet you on the tarmac. Do not unload!"

"Affirmative," the pilot said and pulled back on the power and adjusted the autopilot for a gentle descent to five thousand feet. He wasn't sure he would still be able to land the plane, but was forcing himself to fly the plane; he was weak, eyes watering, headache and body aches all over. His copilot had passed out; and the head steward was sitting in the jump seat behind him, with a cold towel doing what she could to keep him awake. She hurt and could barely control herself, but did what she could to keep the pilot from passing out.

"Sarah, thank you, if we make… it through this… I owe you dinner," the pilot stumbled through his speech.

"Mack, you owe me more than that," Sarah responded before she threw up on the floor; they were out of bags. Thirty-five minutes later, the pilot landed the plane and taxied off the runway. Once cleared, he shut down; and they waited for the rescue vehicles to arrive. The pilot passed out as soon as he stopped the plane.

Unknown to the medical team or airport authorities at the time, they had just stopped a major epidemic from spreading throughout the city by quarantining the plane and all of its passengers.

Michelle Dietrich had become sick on board and was taken to the hospital with the other passengers. The strain of virus was discovered after extensive research with the help of several excellent forensic experts. It took over a week to clear up the virus, declare the passengers safe to return to society and release them from the hospital.

Chapter 15 Washington D.C.

"Mr. Sanford, this is Doctor Dobrinski down at Walter Reed; are you coming down this way anytime soon?" He paused for a moment for Sanford to speak and then concluded, "Good, stop by my office as soon as you get here." He hung up the phone; while sitting at his desk, he slowly rotated to look out the window behind him and sat deep in thought. Things at the hospital were not going very well for a lot of people. He had heard about the sick on Flight 854 in New York and thought it was possibly another attack on the United States using biological warfare.

An hour and half after Doctor Dobrinski talked to Sanford, there was a light knock on his office door. "Come in," he called out.

"Doctor, you asked me to stop by, what's up?" Sanford asked as he entered the small, but well appointed, office.

"Yes, yes, please have a seat," Dobrinski said as he pointed to the only chair in the room that did not have books or papers stacked on it. "I am troubled with the condition of the President. His condition is not improving and there is no reason why. His blood pressure is strong, heart is strong, white cells and red cells are in perfect alignment, temperature is normal, pupils are not dilated, but he is getting weaker, skin is very pale, not his normal almost tan look, he is as white as a ghost. It's almost like his body is already dead and starting to decompose, but his internal parts are still in perfect condition. I also believe he has been poisoned. With what, I don't know, something slow acting; and it is eating him from the outside."

"Damn, that does not sound good."

"No, it is not good. If we can't reverse it in the next couple of days, he will be just bones and internal organs; and his muscles, skin and external body parts will be gone."

"Can he speak?"

"No, only mumbles; his skin is so brittle that when he tries to talk, he starts to bleed. So I told him not to talk; we keep feeding him liquids and antibiotics with hopes that it will reverse."

"Is there anything I can do to help you? Specialist, whatever. We have the best in the world here at Walter Reed, but there may be someone out there that could help," Sanford offered.

"I am looking for someone out there that may know what kind of poison was used on him and have an antidote or at least know how to reverse it."

"Okay. I am going back to the White House to brief the VP and decide who else needs to know," Sanford said and then stood and turned heading for the door.

"Mr. Sanford, I will call you if his condition changes, or if I can find anyone that knows what has caused this."
"Call on my cell and just ask to stop by; don't say anything on the phone about his condition. We need to keep this under wraps for a while longer," Sanford said and got a nod from the doctor.

"Did you hear about American Airlines Flight 854? Seems they had a plane full of very sick passengers. Came out of Berlin, could it be another attack?"

"Possibly, we are looking into it. The passengers are being interviewed and one stands out as a suspect," Sanford said. Forty minutes later, Sanford was sitting across from the Vice President. He had just briefed him on the President's condition and what they had learned about the American Airlines flight.

"Mr. Sanford, now that is a serious problem. What are we going to do? I don't want to run the country, but will if I have to. I would prefer Mitchell sitting in this office. I have two more space projects that need my attention prior to launch. We were lucky with the launch of Star Wars and Star Wars II but this one is super critical for the defense of our nation. I guess I can still monitor from here."

"Yes, I know, Star Wars Three and Four need to be up and operational; so between you and me, we will run the country. That is why Darrell hired me in the first place. Our biggest problem is finding out who poisoned him. We need to bring CIA and FBI in the loop; maybe, with their help, we can find out who poisoned him."

"Right, call them and get them over here as soon as possible. It is two twenty now; let's get them in here at three thirty," Vice President Mike Bell said quietly, unsure of his ability to run the country. He was a scientist, engineer and designer of space based weapon systems. He had no idea how to run a country.

Chapter 16 Over the Atlantic

After filing a Trans Atlantic International flight plan, they took off at four in the afternoon. The take off was smooth and the weather was partly cloudy with a chance of rain later in the evening, but they would be way gone by the time the rain moved in.

"Mr. Pierce and Mr. Randal, here are your drinks; dinner will be served shortly. Would you prefer steak or chicken?" Mary said as she set down a couple of cold beers in front of each of them.

"Steak for me, Mary, and thanks," Josh replied.

"Me too, Mary, and thanks," Davin agreed.

"It will be about fifteen minutes. Okay?"

"Fine, as long as Captain Blair up there doesn't spill our beer, I will be happy," Davin commented.

"I heard that, Pierce; be careful, it could get a little choppy up here. The weather is moving in faster than predicted. Keep your seat belts buckled," Blair stated over the intercom.

"Here are your steaks, gentlemen. Is there anything else I can get you before I take dinner up to our drivers?" Mary said as she set down their meals. After getting a no from both of them, she headed back to the galley to get the crew meals together. They would eat the same thing as Davin and Josh with the exception of the beer. Well, Mary might have a beer if she wanted it, but she decided she did not.

Cruising at thirty-eight thousand, feet, the air was thin and smooth as glass. There were several cumulus nimbus clouds building up on the horizon just to the north of them; nothing to worry about; they would be long past them before they would become a factor.

Up front in the cockpit, dinner had been served and enjoyed by both the crew. "Watch the temp on number one, seems to be climbing a bit," Blair instructed his copilot. "Yeah, about twenty degrees hotter than normal."

"GPS says we are at almost half way across," Blair stated and then looked closely at the moving chart to see where the nearest land was. There was no land within a thousand miles of their location.

"Cap, number one is red lining!"

"Shut her down!" Blair ordered and then reached behind his seat and grabbed the emergency manual and flipped to the heading for water landings. They still had an engine running strong and could make it to Madrid on one, just a little slower."

"Flame out on number 1."

"Good, radio approach and inform them we have a problem." Blair ordered.

"Cap, we have a problem, number 2 is starting to overheat."

"Euro approach, this is Gulfstream five niner six approximately twelve hundred miles out with engine trouble," the copilot called. He received no response even after numerous attempts.

"No joy, Cap. Switching transponder to emergency code," Blair said and then pressed the IDENT button, which indicated to the Air Traffic controller who, where and at what altitude they were flying, and that they were declaring an emergency.

"Flame out, number two," the copilot announced.

"Buckle up back there; we have a major problem and are going down. Mary, prepare for an emergency water landing. Both engines have flamed out, and we are not able to restart; we are going down," Blair reported over the intercom as calmly as he could in this situation.

Immediately, Josh and Davin stood and moved to the cockpit. "Are you serious?"

"Serious as a heart attack; we have not been able to contact anyone. Both engines have quit; I suggest getting strapped in and put on your vests. If you need anything of importance, you best have it on you when you exit this bird; she is dead, and we have about fifteen minutes till impact with the water. And it is going to be tricky; there is a dark storm on the horizon; ocean is probably rough. Mary, get the raft out of the closet and put on your vest. Now get back there; I have work to do!"

Chapter 17 French Connection

Joanne Morgan, aka Mi-Cha Sang, walked into CIA Headquarters at 5:30 in the evening after flying all night and most of the day to reach Washington as quickly as possible. She was tired, confused and mad, because her cover had been compromised; and she had no idea how or when it happened. Ordered to report directly to Ashley Peterson as soon as she arrived, she walked quickly up to the front of the building. Using her identification card, she entered the building and was stopped by a guard before getting more than twenty feet inside.

"Ms. Morgan, Ms Peterson is expecting you; please come with me," the guard insisted as he turned and walked over to a private elevator in the corner of the lobby. He pressed the button and waited; Joanne stood nervously beside him. Moments later, the door opened and they both stepped inside. He pressed the button for B-2, meaning the second level basement.

"I know the way, and I am cleared to be here. You don't have to escort me," she stated.

"Yes I do. You are not going to Ms Peterson's office; she is in a meeting in the main conference room and you are to go there."

"I know where it is."

"I have been ordered to escort you; sorry, Ms Morgan," the guard stated and waited for the door to reopen in the basement. It opened and standing there were two armed guards. They were not smiling.

"Ms Morgan, please come with us; Ms Peterson is expecting you," the tallest one said and then he turned and started walking down the long hallway. The second armed guard remained at the elevator while the guard that brought her down pressed the lobby button to return upstairs. Minutes later, her escort stopped in front of a door, knocked once and then turned the handle and opened the door, pushing it open so she could enter. He did not go in.

"Morgan, glad you are alright; we have a lot to discuss. Please help yourself to something to eat and drink and take a seat," Ashley Peterson said as soon as the door closed behind Morgan. "Sorry about the guard thing, but we needed you down here as soon as you got here. Not roaming around the halls looking for me."

"No problem, Ms Peterson."

"Call me Ashley; now if Mr. Sanford would just get here, we could start."

"My cover was compromised; how did it happen?" Morgan asked.

"That is a good question; we may have a mole in our midst. We are still trying to uncover that. But you were not the only one compromised. Three of our field operatives are now dead and two others have just returned to home plate. But we will cover all that and more as soon as…" Ashley was saying just as the door opened and Mr. Tony Sanford walked in.

"Sorry for being late; we have a serious problem at the White House which I will brief you on in private. Ms Morgan would you step out for a moment? I need to bring Ashley up to speed. Just wait in the hall for a moment; I will get you when we are done."

"Sure," she replied and stepped out the door. Once it closed, Sanford briefed Ashley on the President's condition and asked for assistance in finding out by whom and how he was poisoned. Ashley agreed and would advise as to who would be working on it, if she did not do it herself.

"Wait, why not put Morgan on this; she is capable and right now doesn't have an assignment."

"Sure, she can be read into this."

"Good let her in," Ashley said to Sanford.

"You can come back in Ms Morgan," Sanford said as he stuck his head out the door to get her.

"Joanne, we have a new assignment for you. It is a continuation of your search for General Shin. We received a tip that General Shin is in France. You are going to fly there to assist in his capture and arrest. Don't unpack; we will set up a flight for you. Can you leave tomorrow?"

"Yes, just need to repack with some different clothing; what I have in my bag just will not do in France," Joanne replied.

"Good. Before you fly to France, we need you to question the President's doctor about his condition and any information on his recovery time," Ashley said and continued with briefing Joanne and Tony about what they knew of General Shin and his movements.

Chapter 18 White House Press Meeting

"Good evening Ladies and Gentlemen, the Vice President will be out in a minute or two to cover tonight's briefing. Before you ask where the President is, I will answer that right now. The President is presently in Walter Reed hospital undergoing his annual physical. He is doing fine; but since he was recently rescued after being held captive, the doctors wanted to make sure he is in good health. He should be back in the White House by the end of the week. Now please be patient; the VP will be out… wait, here he is now. Ladies and Gentlemen, may I introduce the Vice President of the United States, Michael Bell."

"Good evening, sorry for my delay; Mr. Sanford, our National Security Advisor, stopped me in the hall to give me an update on a matter we are working on. But you are here to learn about our efforts against ISIS, our space program, and of course our recovery programs for the country. So let me begin with telling you that President Mitchell has authorized additional money for the recovery of the country. The military reserves have been extended to help protect the public; martial law has been dropped in all states except California, and that should be lifted soon. Most of the infrastructure has been recovered; our

Cyber Command at McDill Air Force Base was severely damaged by the terrorists from North Korea. They did lose several key personnel and their building was completely destroyed. But they were able to recover the infrastructure and have started to rebuild the computer software that was compromised, which caused the failure of the systems. The only survivor, a Korean female, is in custody, I cannot say anything else about that at this time due to the ongoing investigation." He paused for a second to take a sip of water. "I cannot go into details, but the CIA and FBI are tracking a group of terrorists that may be behind the attacks on our country. We will give you more information when we can release it, but understand that it is an ongoing investigation and we cannot discuss it at this time. That is all I have for now. Oh, President Mitchell is resting and taking a needed break; his annual physical should be over in a day or two and he will be back here. Any Questions?" After a brief pause the VP asked, "Mr. Blackstone, *United Press*, what's on your mind?"

"Vice President Bell, we lost a lot of good people in the attacks, the nuclear explosions in Boston and Denver. The recovery is long and extensive; I know Congress and the Senate lost a lot of good people also. I also know that just making appointments to Congress and the Senate is not possible, but elections are not for two more years. Is the administration planning on holding elections soon?"

"Good question, Mr. Blackstone. That subject has come up several times and no decision has been made as yet. We are waiting a bit longer, at least until we have been able to restore the country back to almost normal. True, we cannot ever be normal with two nuclear hot areas within our boundaries. That is not saying that each state should not hold elections to pick the candidate they would like to represent them in Congress and the Senate to fill the spaces that have become vacant. When the states feel they are ready, they can hold their elections. But we will not dictate when they will have to be; we will not install new members for at least the next eight months. Next question."

"Mr. Vice President, Anne Smith, *Washington Post*. Is it true that there is a secret underground facility that is used to house the government in case of war similar to the one that was exposed on the Discovery Channel two years ago?"

"Ms Smith, that would be great if there were one; and yes, the one that was located in one of our largest hotels is no longer used but could be put back into use with a little work. But an underground facility, no, sorry, we only wish. Next question."

"Vice President Bell, Mike Broderick, *LA Times*, we have been told that the nuclear fallout has drifted out to sea. My question is, with the cloud heading east, do we have to worry about our friends in Europe, England and other countries in line of the cloud?"

"The scientists are working on that as we speak. And to answer your question, I would only have to speculate and say that with luck the cloud will dissipate and all the radiation will end up in the ocean. Of course that could cause other problems, but they are running scenarios and planning for the worst. I have time for one more question. Yes, Ms Fisher."

"Vice President Bell, as you know, I am with the *Dallas Tribune* and we are curious down in Texas if the government is actively looking for the terrorists that did this to us?"

"As I said earlier, the CIA and FBI have identified an ISIS group that was responsible for several attacks and they are, ah, let me put it this way, they are no longer a problem," the VP stuttered, stumbling over his words. Not knowing exactly how to put it, he knew the ISIS group was located and eliminated earlier in the week by British and American troops.

"Do you mean they have been killed?" Ms Fisher asked quickly.

"I mean to say they are no longer a threat and I cannot comment any more on the subject at this time," Vice President Bell said and then, "That's all for now. Thank you." He turned to leave just as several more questions were being asked.

Chapter 19 Swimming with the Sharks

"Mayday! Mayday! This is Gulfstream November five niner six, total engine failure; we are going down, MAYDAY! MAYDAY!" the copilot kept repeating over the radio and received no response. It was almost as if he were not transmitting at all.

"Try the second comm radio," ordered Captain Blair as he attempted to restart the engines and put the jet into its best glide path which would give them best distance and longevity of flight. He estimated they had about ten minutes before they hit the water. "Mary, is the cabin secure for a water landing?"

"Yes, sir, are we really going to crash?" she asked, a worried look on her otherwise beautiful face.

"We are if the engines don't restart. Pack a bag and get Pierce and Randal to gather any classified stuff and secure it, or pack a bag," he replied attempting to put some humor in his voice but failing completely.

"They are ready; we all have our vests on and the raft is near the door. Each has packed a small bag with weapons and whatever they could put in it. We are ready," she answered.

"Okay, go strap in; we have about seven minutes of flight left, and it is dark which may require some quick turns close to the water so we don't ram into the side of a wave. It could be rough," Blair said calmly, as if he had done this before; and in reality he had, but not for many years and it wasn't an executive jet. As a Navy pilot in Viet Nam, his F-4 Wild Weasel had been severely damaged, but he had been able to nurse his damaged fighter to the coast and set her down in the ocean. But that had been during daylight and it was only he and his Electronic Warfare operator in the back to contend with. This was much different; his executive jet may have been about the same weight, but she was bigger and it was a night landing in an unknown sea.

"Hang on back there we are about to…" he yelled and then banked his jet abruptly to the left to line up with the rolling sea. Luckily, he was able to level the wings in time to let her settle in between the rolling waves. He slowly pulled back on the control yoke until he felt the tail just touch the water; within a second, the wings hit the water and they slid to a stop.

"Open the door and get that raft out, NOW!" Blair yelled and then looked at his copilot and said, "OUT, now!"

Seconds after the big jet skidded over the dark ocean, she started to sink and Davin, Josh, and Mary had the door open and the raft out. Mary grabbed a small waterproof bag and two cases and tossed them into the raft.

"Davin, grab the briefcase!" Josh yelled as he headed for the door.

"I got it," Davin replied and exited the jet.

"What's so important about that briefcase?" she questioned as she slid to the far end of the raft holding her waterproof bag tightly.

"Electronic equipment needed to locate our target," Josh said without saying much more.

"Okay."

The copilot did not hesitate; un-strapping, he stood and heading aft to exit the sinking plane. By the time Blair got to the door, he could see Pierce, Randal, Mary and his copilot sitting in the raft with water slopping around their feet. She was going down slowly.

"We need to get away from her or we could be sucked down with the plane when she starts to go," Blair yelled. With the one paddle, they started paddling briskly away; they watched as their transportation slowly slipped below the surface. Blair reached over and turned on the small light mounted on the side of the raft.

"It is eight forty at night and we are somewhere in the middle of the Atlantic Ocean; what's the plan boss?" Davin asked his partner Randal.

"Well, let's see. We are still alive, which is good; we have rations for how many days, Captain?"

"With five of us, we will have rations for about four days. And you have to know, we were not able to contact anyone before we landed. They do not know we are in the water. But when we don't arrive per our flight plan, they will, hopefully, put out an alert to locate us. And quite possibly organize a search. Keep in mind, and I don't want to make this sound worse than it is, but you need to know. We are not near any shipping lanes, or normal flight paths of commercial flights. It could take days before a ship could get here, unless we get lucky and have a Navy boat nearby. But if we did, they would have answered our distress call, which they did not."

"Now you have really ruined my whole day," Josh commented, shaking his head. "Davin did the case make the trip okay?"

Davin opened the case and poured out several cups of salt water. After considering it for a moment, he decided not to attempt to turn it on until if dried out. "Not sure, Josh. Got a lot of salt water in it, may have fried it. Let's give it time to dry out and then see."

"Not to worry, Josh. What could be better? We are enjoying warm weather, and can work on our tans during the day and sleep all night. And I did throw in a couple of six packs and some tequila," Mary commented quietly.

"I can see it now, the headlines, 'Five rescued after plane crash; all were severely intoxicated which leads the FAA to question whether their drinking caused the crash.' Well anyway, pass me a beer," Josh commented.

"What is that thing, Davin?" Blair asked looking over at the controls and meter within the case.

"Without going into too much detail and without getting you the proper clearances, all you need to know right now is that it is a tracking device and right now it is toast, very soggy toast," Davin commented and closed the lid, spinning the combination lock to secure it. It's not that he didn't trust everyone in the raft, but they did not need to know everything about the mission or the brief case.

"Yeah, pass me and Henry a beer too; Mary, you may as well have one too, it has been one hell of a day and a cold beer would be just great right now," Blair said, taking the beer from Davin as he passed them out.

"Just water for me, I don't drink," Henry stated.

"More for us, your loss," Davin commented and passed Henry a bottle of water.

"So how far is it to any land?" Mary asked.

"The closest land is about one thousand four hundred miles east of us, one thousand six hundred miles to the west, and you can forget going north or south. The current here will probably move us south slowly. We were over half way there and the current will be flowing south as we get closer to the western coast of Portugal and Africa."

"At least we would not be going to colder waters for a while anyway," Josh commented and leaned back and sipped his beer. "We may want to consider getting out of these wet clothes and put on some dry ones."

"Good idea, but I didn't have time to pack; did either of you remember to grab some dry clothes for your pilot and copilot?" Davin agreed and then asked.

"Oops, no, if fact, we did not grab anything for us either. Mary did you?"

"Yes I did, so I would like to pull up the cover so I can change. Please don't look while I change. I am a trained agent and have a good chance of throwing you overboard," she said and then opened her waterproof survival bag and removed a pair of pants and a shirt. Josh pulled up the roof and placed it so it would be a divider between the men and Mary, allowing her to change into dry clothes without worry.

Chapter 20 The Factory

"Dietrich," Gregory answered his cell phone on the fourth ring; he had just walked into his office and was considering having a drink from his wet bar located on the north wall. It was late, just after midnight; he had not planned on being here, but he had just returned from the factory where he completed his briefing. His people were fired up and ready to rule the world; they had their orders and felt that they could not be stopped.

"Gregory, this is Hans."

"Where have you been?" Gregory asked, and walked around behind his desk and sat down.

"I am in Madrid; we are refueling, and I should be in Berlin in a couple of hours. Can we meet?"

"Yes, don't come to the office; I will meet you at the factory. Can you be there by nine in the morning?"

"Good, I will see you there. Good night," Gregory said and then cut the connection. *'Damn, he can link me to the attacks in America, I can't let that happen'* he said to himself as he looked around his office.

Gregory unlocked his desk and removed a file folder. He scanned through it for a couple of seconds, replaced it in the drawer, and then relocked it.

At eight thirty the next morning, Gregory Dietrich walked into his factory. Nothing had ever been built in the factory. Instead, the place had been used to convert normal people into Nazi supporters. And business was good; he and his senior Nazi supporters had converted thousands of young men and women into hard core Nazis. Today would be different; he was to meet with Hans Bormann, his trusted lieutenant, who had been captured, yet escaped and now had returned to the nest. What was he going to do with him? He had been replaced and the Americans knew who he was and what he looked like; this was a liability.

Walking up to the stage, Gregory turned and sat on the edge waiting for Hans to arrive. He did not have long to wait. At precisely eight fifty-five, Hans entered the factory via the side door; it was the only one that he could enter through as the rest were barred from the inside. The side door had a combination lock on it and only a few trusted members knew the combination.

"Hans, my old friend, how are you?" Gregory asked as Hans walked across the tiled floor.

"I am fine, Gregory, how are you?"

"I am doing fine. I am so happy you are safe and have returned. We have a problem which you are uniquely qualified for. Are you interested?" Gregory asked as Hans approached.

"Gregory, I don't know what happened, I have no idea how they were able to find me."

"Water under the bridge, Hans, let us concentrate on the future. Are you sure nobody followed you here?"

"I discovered I was being followed, but took care of them in Bermuda. Their plane should have already crashed in the ocean, and they will never be found. They had landed within two hours after I had. I found out they were asking questions around the airport and talked to the pilot that flew me to Panama City. They were good enough to locate the flight I took out of Panama City and followed me to Bermuda, but I had already met with some of our contacts and had them sabotage their plane. They would get about fifteen hundred miles out of Bermuda before both their engines would fail and they would crash. Their radios would also fail about the same time. During refueling, our man had placed a device onboard that would send a signal to their engine control module indicating an overheating problem. The system would cause the engines to shut down and not start again.

116

The device would also disable their radios and navigation system. In other words, they would have a total electrical failure while over a thousand miles from land and no way to communicate. Flight control centers do not have radar out that far so they would not know if they were still flying or crashed. They will not bother us again."

"Good, that was good thinking, Hans. But they will be missed and search and rescue operations will occur. . However, they may never be found, just like many other planes and ships that enter that area."

"For now we are clear of them," Hans commented.

"Okay, you were not here last night; we had a full house and assignments were made and the teams are moving to their posts. The war has started and we need everybody working together to make this successful."

"What do you want me to do?" Hans asked anticipating a juicy assignment, maybe going back to America to direct the operations.

"Hans, I can't send you back to America; they have your picture and you would not make it past airport security or immigration at any port. We would have to smuggle you in and that would be risky for you and the men doing the smuggling. So

I have decided that your usefulness has run its course, sorry Hans you have been a good soldier," Gregory said as he pulled his Luger 9mm pistol from its holster and pointed it at Hans. "Sorry Hans." He shot Hans in the head, replaced his Luger in its holster, walked over to where Hans had fallen dead and stepped over his body. Gregory walked over to a fifty-five gallon drum and dropped in a match which immediately lit the flammable material he had placed there before the meeting. He removed his gloves, dropped them in the barrel, and then proceeded to leave the building, switching off the lights as he left.

Ten minutes later, he climbed into his car which was parked about a mile away and drove back to Berlin, eighty miles from the factory.

Chapter 21 Southern France

General Jin-Ho Shin returned to his Villa in southern France around midnight that night to find his friend dead on the floor and his friend's wife missing.

After reaching inside his coat pocket, he pulled out his cell phone and dialed the local police to report the murder and kidnapping of his friend's wife. Twenty minutes later, the police arrived. He let them in and the questions started which he answered to the best of his ability. He had nothing to hide. He was not guilty, and he needed help to find his friend's wife. After about an hour, the police detective told the General he would have to stay at a hotel while they did their work in the villa, hoping to discover who killed the doctor and kidnapped his wife.

"Detective, I will be staying at my villa in Cannes; this villa was the doctor's and his wife's. I was just visiting."

"Okay, leave your address and phone number with the Sergeant when you leave, thank you; and please don't leave the country," the detective said and returned to his investigating.

The villa had been searched by professionals; and after looking around, he left and headed for his car. His driver was waiting and opened the rear door of his car. Minutes later, they pulled out of the driveway and headed toward the city.

At the same time they pulled out, a dark BMW sedan with two members of the CIA team that had penetrated the Villa earlier also started moving. They had been waiting since the raid that they had assisted in at eight that evening. They pulled out at a safe distance behind the Bentley that the General was riding in.

"Where to, sir?" the General's driver asked as they left the villa.

"My villa in Cannes, please," the general said and kicked off his shoes. He was wondering who had kidnapped his friend's wife and killed the doctor.

The BMW maintained a distance behind the Bentley of about a half mile. The driver, John Polson, looked at his partner and said, "Wonder what is going through his mind right now."

"Not sure, but I would dare to guess he is wondering who invaded the villa and killed his friend and kidnapped his wife," Amber Miller, Secret Service Agent on temporary assignment with the CIA, replied. "Did you get that tracking device on the Bentley?"

"Yeah, that was the easy part. You had the hard part in distracting the driver for a couple of minutes."

"Not a problem, a few unbuttoned buttons on my blouse and my tight pants made it easy. He was so busy concentrating on my cleavage that he never saw you on the other side of the Bentley. By the way, that is one very nice car, probably cost a half million."

"At least that, maybe more," John Polson, Senior Secret Service Agent on temporary duty with the CIA Covert Operations commented as they drove. "Better contact Team Two and let them know that they will need to pick up the track in a couple of miles. We need to turn off, or they will notice they are being followed."

"Right," Amber said and then reached into her purse and pulled out her secure SAT phone and called Team Two alerting them to pick up the tail and gave them a location.

"We will switch cars and pick them up near Cannes."

"Are you sure that is where they are going?" Amber questioned.

"Yes, HQ discovered that he owns a villa in Cannes and the doctor owned the one in Marseille," Polson responded.

"Where are we going?"

"The airport; we need to fly ahead to catch up in Cannes," Polson said and then asked, "Is Team Two in place?"

"Yes."

"Good, lets head for the airport," Polson said and then turned off the highway and headed toward the airport.

"I will call ahead and let the pilots know we are on the way, Amber said and then dialed the pilot of the waiting CIA corporate jet.

Chapter 22 Cannes, France

"There he is," John Polson said to his partner Amber.

"Right on time; when do want to take him?"

"We need to find out who paid him," Polson stated, "And to do that, we need to do one of two things: one, arrest him and make him tell us. That may be difficult. Or two, tap his phone, bug his villa and computer and watch him until he makes a mistake. This will take time and a lot of effort. What do you suggest, my young Padawan?"

"I suggest the bugging route; we wait until he leaves again; break in, bug the place and monitor for a couple of days, and see what happens. If nothing, then arrest him and make him talk. Force it out of him. He is a terrorist, right!" Amber commented looking at the General's car enter a large gated home located on the coast of France.

"Wow, nice digs," Polson said as they drove by the home watching the gate close automatically. He continued on down the street, made an illegal U turn, and then pulled over under a couple of large shade trees to watch the villa. After picking up his radio, he switched to secure mode and then called to their back up operators, "Team Two and Three, this is One."

"Yes, what you got, One?" the reply came over almost immediately.

"We are parked about a block away from the General's villa; we will be here for the next three hours and then need food; Two, you will replace us. Three, get some rest; we will be going in to bug the villa after dark. Two, bring the toys."

"Roger that, One. We have them in the back of the van. See you this afternoon."

"Which van do you have?"

"Satellite TV installer."

"Good," Polson said, broke the connection, looked over at Amber, and said, "Got your sneakers on?"

"Yes, and you can see that I am dressed for night operations," she said looking down at her clothes, black slacks, tan blouse and her shoes; well, she needed to change those; low heels would not work for these night maneuvers. "I have a black blouse and black sneakers in my backpack. I came prepared, did you?" she asked as she looked at John in his three piece suit, white shirt and black tie, looking more like the Men in Black or a new CIA or FBI agent.

"I have my Go bag in the back and will be ready well before we have to do a 'B' and 'E'," he said referring to a Break and Entry.

Waiting was the hardest part; it was four in the afternoon, and the sun would not go down for another two hours. Their location was good; there was very little traffic on this road as it only serviced the eight villas and then dead ended. The General's villa was third from the last on the ocean side of the street and the other two on the ocean side were under construction. There was no work being done on those this weekend, limiting the traffic even more. There was a nature preserve across the street and no homes at this end of the street. The nearest home across the street was located about fifty yards off the road and almost one hundred yards up the road from the General's. He had chosen well, if he wanted privacy. Their car could not be seen from the villa because of the high wall that surrounded it. They felt safe; and unless the General left the home via boat, his only exit was the front gate.

And so they waited; at 7 p.m., a Satellite TV truck rolled up and stopped across the street from Polson's black BMW.

"Evening boss," the Team Two lead said as he walked up to the sedan.

"Did you bring food?" Polson asked as he stepped out of the car.

"Yeah, pizza; go figure, good Italian pizza here in southern France," he said and handed Polson a *Pizza Hut* box.

"*Pizza Hut*, where did you find this?"

"They are all over the place down here, along with *McDonalds*, *Burger King*, all the fast food joints we have at home are here."

"Well, hell, what did you get us?" Amber asked as she walked around the back of the car, "I am starving." Then she took the box, set it on top of the car, opened it and took out a slice. "Damn this is good."

"Thanks, have you got the gear ready?" Polson said and took a slice for himself.

"Yeah, what's the plan?"

"Simple plan, slip in after dark, bug the house and slip out; we all go in. Bring your side arm; hopefully we will not need them, but, as they say, I would rather have it and not need it than to not have it and need it."

"Good point. It should be dark in an hour; I will put the bugs in four separate bags."

"The villa is two stories, no basement. I was able to tap into the building plans in the city archive while we were waiting and downloaded the floor plans; I will transmit them to your tablets. We should be able to enter from the ocean side, no wall back there; and if he is like most people of France, he will not have locked the back door. Let's hope anyway. If he has, well, we will deal with it at that time. According to the city plans, the home is alarmed and has CCTV, possibly infrared; we can use our night vision goggles to move around."

"John, look," Amber said between bites and watched as the Bentley exited the villa. "Is he in the car or not?"

"Can't tell, the windows are heavily tinted. I could not tell if he was in the back or not. Were you able to see?" Polson asked Team Two.

"No."

"Guess we still go in after dark and take our chances; maybe he went to dinner," Amber stated and continued to eat her pizza and take sips of soda. "After dark, I will walk down to the gate to see if there any lights on inside."

"Good idea. Finish your pizza; we have work to do," Polson commented.

"Polson, I noticed on the way here that they had a security sign in front of the gate, like the ones for ADT we have in the states. We have some equipment in the van that may help," Team Two lead said.

"Okay, tell me more."

"Well, if they have a wireless security system, we should be able to find and disarm it, and if they have video, we can actually see what they are seeing."

"Cool, let's take a look," Polson said excitedly. Minutes later, Brian, Team Two lead, was sitting at a console in the van scanning Wi-Fi signals. Within a few minutes, he was able to narrow down the signal to the villa.

"Wow, they do have video; let's take a look."

"Is this stuff legal?" Amber asked.

"Not exactly stuff you can buy at your *Radio Shack* or online. Special custom built for us; and yes, the technology is classified; and no, it is not exactly legal for most people to do this; but we are not most people," Brian acknowledged. "The house looks empty or at least the public areas; should not be any cameras in the bedrooms or baths. Now that would be illegal."

"Okay, J.P., we should get ready. Looks like this will be easy, in and out quickly," Amber said and then stepped out of the van and walked to the car, opened the trunk and grabbed her bag. Within minutes, she had changed her blouse to a black one, her sneakers were black and she was in the process of putting her hair up in a ponytail.

Chapter 23 Serious Complications

Joanne Morgan, aka Mi-Cha Sang left the conference room confused and worried. Her run in with General Soon-Bok Kim, commander of the North Korean Secret Police had left her shaken from the encounter, but the meeting with Ashley Peterson, Director of CIA left her scared. Somewhere within the bowels of the CIA was a mole, selling secrets and the identities of the field agents. Her career as a field agent may have just ended and possibly even her life.

Joanne headed downstairs to the cafeteria, her pace quickened, and she was not smiling.

"Coffee please, black," she asked the counter attendant.

"Are you okay?" the attendant asked.

"Yes, fine, I am fine, thank you," Joanne responded handing the attendant a five dollar bill and then turned to leave.

"Your change," the attendant almost yelled as Joanne was walking away. Joanne stopped, returned to the counter, and took her change. As she dropped it into her pocket, a couple of coins fell to the floor. She continued to walk to the side door leading to the outside patio. She needed to think and this was the quietest place within the walls of the CIA. Seeing several other people sitting across the patio, she chose a table under a tree away from the other users of the patio.

After finishing her coffee, her nerves were settled and she started to formulate a plan to find out about the President's hospital visit. She stood and walked back into the building and headed for the front door and her car. Forty minutes later, she entered Walter Reed Military Hospital, took the elevator to the security floor, flashed her identification to the guard, and signed in before she walked over to the nurses' station to inquire about the President's doctor.

"I am Joanne Morgan, with the CIA, and I have been asked to talk to the President's personal doctor, is he in?"

"The doctor is in his office. Just a second and I will see if he is busy," the nurse said and picked up the phone to call the doctor. Seconds later she said, "Third door on the left, just knock."

"Thank you, miss," Joanne said and walked down the hall toward the doctor's private office. After knocking, she heard a muffled come in and entered.

"Doctor Dobrinski, I am Joanne Morgan from the CIA. May I ask you some questions about the recent President's visit?

Yes, I know, there are doctor patient privileges, but I have been asked by the Director to check on the President."

"Sure, I will answer what I can; but you rest assured, he's got the best care possible. Ask your questions," Dobrinski said.

"Ok. I am sure you did, but I just want to verify. Did you do a full TOX screening on the President?" she asked.

"We pulled blood as usual and are running the tests as we speak. We should have the results soon. The President is recovering well and there is nothing to worry about," Dobrinski stated, just as there was a knock on the door. "Enter," he yelled and then to Joanne he said, "That should be the TOX screen results."

"Doctor, the results, and they are what you expected," the nurse stated as she walked over and handed the doctor the results.

"Thank you; that will be all," Dobrinski said and quickly opened the folder. His smile immediately disappeared.

"What's wrong doctor?"

"This is not good; according to the test, the President was poisoned which brought on the stroke. Please come with me, now," Dobrinski said as he stood and headed for the door quickly. Joanne stood and followed close behind. "Nurse, come now," he yelled to the Nurses' station.

Quickly walking down the hall, they passed three Secret Service Agents and entered the President's private room.

"Wait here, Ms Morgan," Dobrinski told her.

Twenty-five minutes later, Dobrinski came out of the President's room and was smiling again.

"What happened?" Joanne asked.

"Everything is fine now. We caught it in time. The poison that was used is not toxic until it is mixed with another drug. Then it becomes extremely toxic and within hours it would have killed the President. We have changed his meds and he will be fine. I will not go into all the details, but he will be fine after a couple of days rest."

"Thank you, doctor."

"Do you have any more questions?"

"No, thank you. Please let Director Peterson know if there are any changes," Joanne said and then started for the elevator. The elevator took her down to the parking garage floor; and as the door opened, she was greeted by General Soon-Bok Kim, Commander of the North Korean Secret Police and three

Koreans dressed in suits. Two drew their weapons immediately and pointed them at Joanne.

"Come with me now, Ms Sang, or should I say Ms Joanne Morgan," Kim said quietly.

"And if I refuse?" Joanne questioned.

"You don't want to do that, Ms Morgan. You will not be harmed; we need to talk."

"Ok, let's go."

Chapter 24 Drifting

"Okay, guys and lady, here we are and nobody knows we are down and drifting to who knows where. The radio is not strong enough to reach any land and it will only last about five days broadcasting a mayday and our position. It does have a GPS and it knows where we are, even if we don't. Rations, we have enough for five days if we are careful," Captain Blair calmly said as he outlined their situation and supplies.

"Does it have a fishing rod in there?" Josh asked, hoping.

"Yes, a fishing line and a can of bait, which may prolong our supplies. There are some desalination tablets in here so we could extend our water. And you will be happy to know there are a couple of tubes of sunscreen, which I advise we use, especially you Mary, your fair skin will burn in one day out here. There is a shade cover on the stern; it will cover about half this rubber duck," Blair added.

"Good, we can work on our tans while waiting for someone out there to realize we are missing," Davin said, not sounding very encouraged.

"It is hard to determine which way we are drifting, but my best guess is we are heading south with the current. But with the wind blowing from the south we may be stationary. Now for the best part, our navigation gear on board was erratic at best, almost like it was being jammed or interfered with by some electronic device."

"What are you trying to say, Blair?" Davin asked.

"Well, we may have been several miles off course and I am not sure whether it is north or south of our course; so even if we were able to get a mayday out and give them coordinates, they would likely have been incorrect based on what I was seeing."

"Okay, interesting. So it seems we were sabotaged," Josh deduced and then continued by saying bluntly, "We may be screwed people. We don't know where we are; and they will be looking in an area where we should have been, but we are nowhere near that spot."

"You got that right, old man. We are literally up the creek without a paddle, drifting further away from a search area, which nobody will even get to for several days because we went down miles, possibly hundreds of miles, from our proposed flight plan," Blair commented.

"No, wait; Captain, even if we are a hundred miles south of our track, shouldn't we run into a shipping lane soon?"

"That may be true, but we could be a hundred miles from the nearest shipping lane," Blair said shaking his head.

"Okay, like I said, we may be screwed," Davin commented, as he laid back against the side of the rubber boat. He took a long sip from his now warm beer. "How many more of those do we have?" he asked referring to the beer.

"Just under two cases and four bottles of tequila," Mary replied.

"Good, that should last about a day or two. Don't you think?"

"Sun will be up in about eight hours, so I suggest getting some sleep, if you can," Josh said and then grabbed another beer. "Right after I finish this one."

Davin, Blair, Henry and Mary fell asleep almost right away while Josh nursed his beer and watched the horizon hoping to catch sight of a light from a passing ship or an island, yet knowing full well there were no islands within hundreds of miles of wherever they were and that the possibility of a ship was almost as remote. The night was cool, not cold, but cool, with a light breeze and a half moon glowing high in the sky. Not a

137

cloud could be seen anywhere near, but a few were north of their little boat.

He sipped slowly enjoying every little drop of possibly one of his last beers. He missed Stephanie and worried about her. She would panic when told of the plane crash and would want to send the entire US Navy on a search and rescue mission, but of course did not have the authority to make that happen. The Coast Guard would be dispatched sometime in the morning and immediately head out from Key West and Savannah, Georgia. Several long range aircraft would join in and start a search pattern around their flight path. They would search for four, maybe five, days and then start to scale back, reducing resources and eventually declare all lost at sea.

He knew the scenario well, since he had participated in many S&R events around the world. The chances of locating a tiny rubber boat that had no beacon somewhere in the middle of the Atlantic Ocean was slim at best, especially not knowing for sure where they might have gone down. The search would be a waste of resources. But Josh was always hopeful and very resourceful; between him and Davin, they had gotten out of many close calls. This one might be a little tougher than the rest, but they would survive, at least that was the plan.

Chapter 25 Presidential Concerns

At eight o'clock on Thursday morning, the weather in Washington was cold with light snow and heavy clouds; the temperature was a crisp eighteen degrees Fahrenheit. It was typical weather for February in the northeast and the forecast was more of the same for the next week.

"Mr. Sanford, we need to advise the nation about the President. You first reported that they had found the poison and were able to stop the infection, and now your last report tells me that he may not recover. The doctors are stumped and all treatment seems to be leading them to the same conclusion that I have made. He seems to have relapsed into something more critical, and now, President Mitchell is dying and there is nothing we can do to stop it," Vice President Bell commented during a private meeting with Sanford.

"His daughter, Tara, is with him right now. And I am going over there right after this meeting. But I don't think we should alarm the public just yet. The doctors are doing everything they can and are keeping this under wraps for now. I know that someone may accidently let slip that he is ill; but, I believe, we should keep this quiet for now."

"Against my better judgment, I will concede to your opinion and not say anything yet. But we need to make plans if he should die. Keep in mind; we are operating with only half a Congress and Senate. It could take a little longer to make things happen."

"I understand, Mike. But he is not dead yet; and until he is, he is still the President and should be given every benefit to recover," Tony Sanford said. After a short pause, he added, "I am going over to the hospital and will return in about two hours; I will report to you what I find out as soon as I return." With that Sanford left the Oval Office and headed out of the White House. Driving to Walter Reed Hospital took longer than he had planned. The weather had worsened; snow had increased, and the roads were very slippery. He passed multiple accidents as his driver guided his SUV around the hazards.

"Sir, this snow is becoming a real hazard. Sorry for the delay," his driver commented as he guided the SUV around a parked fire truck.

"Okay, not your fault, Jim," Sanford commented and then pulled his cell phone out of his pocket and dialed the number for Ashley Peterson, Director of CIA. It rang several times before it was picked up.

"Ashley here, how are you doing Tony?" a pleasant voice said when the connection was made.

"Can you meet me for lunch?"

"Sure, where?"

"Your conference room; I will bring lunch."

"Okay, noon."

"See you then," Sanford said and cut the connection just as they pulled into the parking lot of the hospital. "I will be back quickly, Jim, keep the motor running. We need to stop at *Wong's Chinese* to pick up lunch and then over to CIA HQ by noon."

"You want me to run over to *Wong's* to save time?"

"No, I will call our order in; let me know what you want so I can add yours to the order."

"Kung Pao Chicken and ice tea, sweet," Jim responded.

"You got it! Be back in a few minutes; well, as soon as I can," he said. He climbed out of the SUV and almost slipped on the ice as he got out. Minutes later, he was walking down the hall toward the secure area of the hospital where the president was resting comfortably.

"Ah, Mr. Sanford, glad you stopped by; let's go into my office and chat for a minute. The President's daughter is in with him right now, and we don't need to disturb her at the moment,"

Doctor Dobrinski said as he approached Sanford just inside the secure area. "Please have a seat; this will not take long."

"How is he?" Sanford asked as he sat across from Dobrinski.

"President Mitchell's condition is improving, slowly; but we have seen some marked improvement over the past few hours. We don't know why; but maybe, just maybe, his system is starting to reject the poison. We have high hopes that he will fully recover in the next week."

"That is great news, Doctor; but, I know there is always a but. There always is," Sanford questioned.

"His body is recovering, but I am not sure of his mind; he has gone from one severe trauma to another. His mind was slipping while still in the Oval office. I am not sure he is up to the challenge anymore. I would like to bring in a specialist, someone that understands the mind better than you or me."

"Do you have someone in mind?"

"Yes, he is on staff here, but not cleared to treat the President."

"Give me his name. Have you talked with him about this yet?"

"No, wanted to get him cleared first. Can we do that quickly?" Dobrinski asked handing Sanford a small sticky note with the name and phone number of the doctor he wanted to bring on board.

"Thank you, I will get right on it and should have an answer by tomorrow. Is that okay?"

"Yes, that will be fine. If he doesn't check out, let me know; I have a second candidate."

"This one will be fine. I hope," Sanford said and then stood. The doctor stood and they both headed down to the President's hospital room.

Chapter 26 Breaking and Entering

On the coast of southern France is a little town known as Cannes. Once a year, the town grows in size with the Festival De Cannes. Many movie stars, producers, publishers and wannabe actors and movie makers arrive for the Festival De Cannes (known prior to 2002 as the International Film Festival). This festival was created by Jean Zay, Minister for Education and Fine Arts. He was keen on establishing an international cultural event in France that would rival the Venice Film Festival. It was first held in 1939, but the war caused a delay in having another until September 20th, 1946. It was held every September since, except in 1948 and 1950, until it was changed to May in 1952. The Festival De Cannes has been in May ever since.

Luckily the town of Cannes was not very crowded in February; and the sleepy little town boasted a great beach, many excellent restaurants and a very friendly population. The General had purchased a beautiful villa right on the ocean with the money he made for attacking the United States with eight ICBMs.

Polson, Miller and Brian were prepping to enter the villa to plant multiple bugs; but after seeing the security system that was already in place, they were questioning whether they really needed to add more. The security system that was already in the villa provided video and sound to almost every room; the only thing it didn't do was cover the cell phones that most everyone around the world depended on. But Brian had a fix for that too.

"Polson, when he uses his cell phone we will be able to hear what is said."

"Guess we don't need to do a 'B' and 'E' on the villa; glad you brought the toys. This gear is top notch; and sitting here and monitoring is our best bet," Polson said. He then looked over at Amber and said, "Why don't you and I get some real food, and leave Brian and his partner here to monitor."

"Sounds good to me. I could use a good meal; we have been running so fast that we have not had much time to get good food except for that pizza a few hours ago," Amber agreed.

"As we used to say when I was with the Army Security Agency, 'In God we Trust, all others we monitor'," Polson stated as he and Amber left the van. "Continue the good work; we will be back in about an hour or so."

"You got it, boss," Brian said.

"Don't call me boss; I am just on loan to the agency, remember," Polson said and turned to Amber, "Are you going to stay in all black?"

"Yes, here in France, black is formal. Let's go," she replied.

Since the weather was warmer than it was in Washington D.C., they did not need to wear heavy coats but did wear light jackets, mostly to cover the weapons each carried. They left Brian and his team to monitor the villa, drove down the block and turned right at the stop sign. Polson had in mind a nice steak with a cold beer on the side; Amber had a different idea of a hot dinner. So to compromise, they stopped at a small bistro about nine miles from the villa. She had read about the restaurant in the reviews about the Festival de Cannes and thought that he would enjoy it.

After ordering drinks and an appetizer, they sat back to enjoy the atmosphere of the little bistro with its subdued lighting and small tables with checker board table cloths. However, the most interesting item was General Jin-Ho Shin sitting at a table in the corner chatting with young oriental women, possibly Korean, but it was hard to tell with the subdued lighting. What were the chances that they would be sitting in the same restaurant that the man they were following was having dinner in?

"Did you see the Bentley outside, John?"

"No, did you?"

"Yes I did. Wasn't sure it was his because this town has a lot of high priced cars. So I took a chance and it paid off," she replied smiling. "And the tracking device showed me it was his."

Chapter 27 East Berlin Meets the West

Gregory Dietrich arrived at his office in East Berlin at six fifteen local time; the sun had just started to set in the west, figuratively and realistically. His plan to conquer the United States and all her allies had started. By morning, the rest of the United States Senate and Congress would be eliminated, along with any member of the military, police forces, and any opposition his teams would encounter within the capital city of Washington, D.C. It was a huge undertaking, but his people were well trained and would succeed; failure was not an option. He needed to succeed with his plan to take over the world, or he would not live beyond the end of the week.

After reaching for a bottle of red wine he had reserved for this occasion, he slowly opened the bottle, poured himself a tall glass, and then held it up to the light to look at the clarity and richness of his wine. "The world will record tomorrow as the beginning of the end of the United States. This time we will not fail," he said out loud and then turned to see who had entered his office.

"Good evening, General Kim, so happy you could make it. Would you care for a glass of wine?"

"Yes, please, thank you. Gregory," General Soon-Bok Kim replied, as he took the glass of wine.

"What is the status of General Shin?"

"He is in Cannes; I presume he is having dinner about now. The CIA is watching him; my men are watching the CIA; and we are ready to move on your command."

"Everything is in motion; tomorrow morning, the United States and England will wake up to a totally different world."

"Have you heard any reports regarding President Mitchell?" she asked.

"Yes, he is on the road to recovery; thanks to the drug we were able to slip into his I.V. Luckily, we were able to exchange a nurse in the hospital with one of ours. She was able to substitute the I.V. drip with the antidote one. They never knew we had poisoned him, and will never know we saved him too. Pretty slick if I do say so myself. By the way, what was that poison? No, never mind, I really don't need to know."

"In the morning, your men are to eliminate the CIA team watching the villa, remove General Shin and take him to a safe location. Your operative is with him now, correct?"

"Yes, she will ensure he is drugged before bed; and we will move in and remove him from the villa," she commented.

149

"If he gives you too much trouble, kill him," Gregory said with no feelings at all. "How do you like the wine?"

"As you wish, as you wish," she said between sips.

"What about the hooker?"

"She will be long gone before you get there; once he is asleep she is to leave," Dietrich said between sips of his wine.

Twenty minutes later, Soon-Bok Kim left Dietrich's office and headed south toward Cannes. As she was climbing into her car, she did not pay any attention to the man and woman having a drink on the patio of the bistro across the street from Gregory's office building. The couple was not in a hurry; they had watched Kim enter the building; and once she was in the building, the young woman slipped over to Kim's vehicle and placed a tracking device on it.

"Let's wait until she is several blocks away before following. That tracker will transmit up to one hundred miles and the battery is good for a year. Just wish I could have placed one on her; it would help a lot, but I guess that wasn't in the cards."

"Good, I really want to finish my latte and this muffin," her partner said.

"Eating too many of them will put twenty pounds on you. Better watch out, the company has a weight reduction program which you will not like."

"I know, but once in a while you have to eat the sweet stuff just to remind you how good it tastes, and how bad it is for you. This is my reminding time," he responded and took another bite. "How's the signal on the tracker?"

"Strong, she is heading west toward what used to be the wall. Probably going to cross over to the autobahn and then head south to Cannes. I assume she is going to Cannes, but we will know shortly, won't we?" she said and then continued, "I wish we could have heard that conversation between Kim and Dietrich."

"Would have been good, but there was no way of getting into his office; and he has sound suppression equipment running in there to keep anyone with a snooper mike from listening in from outside. I tried to listen, but only got garbage," he said.

"Wonder what they are up to?"

Chapter 28 Sunrise Over the Atlantic Ocean

Morning broke without a sound except for the lapping of the waves on the sides of their rubber boat. The sun rose slowly in the east; and within minutes, everyone was awake on the little orange rubber boat, everyone except Henry. It seemed he could sleep through most anything; at least that is what everyone thought. Reaching over Henry, Blair pulled up the half cover to provide shade for Henry and anyone else that wanted to escape the sun. Henry rolled over and started to snore.

"Damn, he can sleep through most anything, can't he?" Josh said looking over at Henry.

"Let him be, we need to conserve our strength. Anyone hungry?" Davin asked.

"Sure, I will have two eggs, over easy, three pieces of bacon, crispy, and hash browns," Josh said expecting to get a laugh but only got stares. "A person could hope. Okay, I will take whatever is available."

"Here, MRE brown bag. Enjoy," Blair said as he pitched Josh a Meal Ready to Eat (MRE) in a light brown bag, not looking to see what it was. The rations provided with their little orange rubber boat were MREs which provided the most nourishment in the least amount of room. The MREs came with everything you needed: main course, side dish, dessert, and a powdered drink. They were much better than the C or K rations or earlier MREs that were the staple of World War II, Viet Nam and Desert Shield/Storm. Feeding the military in the field was difficult at the best of times. So over time C and K rations were improved; and with the creation of MREs, they were the latest and best product to keep soldiers in the field fed and nourished properly. Many survival schools, life raft manufacturers and other civilians had also started stock piling MREs as a survival food that would last for years.

"Thanks, spaghetti and meat balls, my favorite," Josh commented as he cut open his breakfast.

"Well, day one begins; after breakfast, I want to look at the distress beacon and radio to see if I can boost the range," Davin said as he opened his MRE.

"First, we need to see if they are at least working," Blair said.

"Yeah, that too," Davin replied as he stuck a fork in the pork and rice meal he had. After finishing his breakfast, he picked up the rescue beacon. With the small tool kit that was supplied with the orange rubber boat, he opened it up and poured out the water that had somehow gotten inside. "No wonder it doesn't work, damn thing is flooded."

"How is the battery?" Josh asked.

Pressing his fingers on both terminals Davin tested the battery. "Ouch, still has power."

"That's a start," Josh agreed.

"Morning everyone, what's for breakfast?" Henry asked as he finally woke up.

"Morning, hell it is almost afternoon and lunch time, which will consist of pizza and beer," Josh responded.

"Good, I will have a slice and two cold beers," Henry came back.

"Here is an MRE, enjoy," Blair said and handed Henry the MRE.

"Mr. Pierce, what you doin'?"

"Attempting to fix the beacon; do you know anything about these things?" Davin asked as he looked inside the back of the transmitter.

"A little, my degree is in communications electronics. Let me take a look. Is the battery still good?"

"Yeah, here, have at it, see what you can do," Davin said as he handed the beacon radio to Henry.

"Maybe we can dry it out; and if nothing is fried, I believe I can make it work. May have to sabotage some of the other electronic gear to fix it, if we have to. What other electronic stuff do we have?"

"Just the comm radio," Davin said.

"No, we also have a small FM radio," Mary added.

"We do?"

"Yeah, it was in my pocket when we crashed, and it did get wet, but maybe we can use parts from it to fix the beacon or transmitter," Mary said as she handed Henry the FM radio.

"Good, I will see what I can do; no promises, but will do my best," Henry said between bites and tinkering with the beacon.

As best they could tell, they were drifting south; but without any source of reference, they could not tell how fast they drifted or how far. At night, they could take a start bearing, if they had a sextant to do so, which they did not have. Blair spent the day with the limited supplies and material he had and fashioned a primitive sextant. He was a highly trained Navy pilot and navigator who upon discharge converted to become a CIA pilot and field operative. Their little orange rubber boat did not come with oceanographic charts, but before leaving their downed plane, he was able to grab his portable tablet which held all the aeronautical charts he required to fly for his job as corporate pilot for the CIA. With any luck, he would be able to at least narrow down their possible location; and if Henry was able to get the radio working, then they might have a chance at surviving.

The sky was clear and blue; the sea was providing a gentle roll of about four feet, which made it easy for the crew of the little orange rubber boat to relax. The sun was warm, verging on getting hot; temperature was in the mid eighties and all seemed well for the survivors. Unknown to them was that a storm was brewing off the coast of Africa; it was more than three hundred miles away, but could cause them some problems in a few days, if it intensified. It was not hurricane season, so there was no worry about that; but a storm at sea could be very dangerous, especially if you were floating around in a small orange rubber boat without a paddle or way to steer.

Chapter 29 Search and Rescue

"This is Coast Guard Cutter *Intrepid*, we are heading zero nine zero at fifteen knots, approximately two hundred miles due east of Bermuda," The captain of the cutter reported to his base in Bermuda. "We are at least a day from the search area. What's the status of the air search?"

"Nothing yet, no oil slick or wreckage seen, they are still on station."

"Good. We will get there as soon as possible."

"Roger, stand by, we just got something." After a long pause from headquarters in Bermuda, they transmitted. "Cutter *Intrepid*, you are ordered to abort search and return to base immediately. Our mission has just changed. The aircraft will continue to search, but you are to report back to Bermuda immediately."

"Understood, what is going on?"

"We are at war and need all forces back at base for further orders."

"Come about; full speed ahead. We have a mission change. War has been declared and we are to report back to base," the captain ordered and then thought for a moment, "Go to red alert, lock and load all weapons. We don't know what is on the horizon and I want to be prepared."

The cutter immediately made an abrupt one hundred eighty degree turn and went to full speed of about twenty-three knots. It still would take a day plus to get back to Bermuda.

Meanwhile, several hundred miles below their intended flight path, a small orange rubber boat bobbed up and down in the rolling ocean. Unknown to the occupants was the fact they were so far away from their intended flight path that the rescue aircraft were searching that they would not be found for weeks. As the sun started to fall, a light MRE dinner and sips of the rationed water were shared. Captain Blair adjusted his home built sextant so he could estimate their approximate position tonight.

"Do you think that will work, Captain?" Henry asked.

"Yeah, better than our radios; any luck with those?" Blair responded.

"No, the beacon has a couple of fried circuits; must have happened when the salt water leaked in. As for the transceiver, well that is another story; I have to see if I can get it to turn on. Could be something simple; but until I get it apart, I can't tell. Even if I can get it to work, it may not have the range we need to communicate with anyone on shore."

"Not good news, Henry. Well, do what you can to fix it. I will find out where we are," Blair said and then looked at Davin and Josh. "Well, guys, our second night of relaxing on the high seas, any beer left?"

"Yeah, we did not drink all of it," Josh said and handed Blair a beer. "Mary, how are you holding up?"

"Well, I could be lying beside a pool or on the beach somewhere where it is warm holding a margarita and dreaming of a massage; but here I am, stuck in a little orange boat, with five of my male friends."

"Could be worse, Mary," Davin said.

"How so?" she questioned.

"We could be out of beer," he responded which got a laugh out of everyone.

Several hours later, the sun had set and the stars were out in all their glory. Captain Blair worked with his home made sextant, constantly looking up at the stars, taking a reading, marking the chart and then checking his sightings. With the primitive sextant, his measurements were not exactly accurate; but he would be within an acceptable distance.

"Well, lady and gentlemen, I believe I have a reasonable location of our little orange boat," Blair stated.

"Don't leave us in suspense old man," Josh said.

"Well, plus or minus about one hundred miles, we are about six hundred fifty miles northwest of Cape Verde. Actually a heading of about one hundred seventy degrees would put us on top of Cape Verde, which would also put us about eight hundred miles west of Western Sahara. But the current will keep us way off shore. With luck, I will be able to verify that in a couple of hours with another reading and determine how fast we are drifting and in which direction we are travelling. So you will have to wait until then to be sure."

"Will you also be able to predict how long it will take to drift down there?" Mary asked.

"Yes, but it will take multiple sightings to be sure. But, as I said, I will have a better answer in a few hours."

Two hours later, Captain Blair started taking more star readings with his home made sextant. He worked and reworked his calculations several times and shook his head as if he did not understand what he was seeing.

"What is it, Blair?" Davin asked.

"We have a problem and I can't explain it," Blair said. "I need to take readings again in a couple of hours to be sure. I really wish our cell phones worked. But without being in a cell zone, the GPS would not even work as you know. I need to verify my readings. ”

"Well?" everyone said in unison.

"Okay, if my readings are reasonably accurate, we have moved about three hundred feet, plus or minus three hundred feet."

"What?"

"Unless I am completely wrong, we are just sitting in one spot and not moving at all. At this rate we will get to Cape Verde in about two years if even then. I need to take more readings in a couple of hours to be sure, so don't panic yet."

"No panic, pass me one of those hot beers, I need a drink," Josh said.

"A shot of tequila would be better, but I will have another beer also. Here, Captain, you look like you need a drink too," Davin said holding out a beer.

"Not now, maybe later," Blair said

"I will take that," Henry said.

"Thought you did not drink, Henry," Blair stated.

"I don't, but I thought it might be a good time to start," Henry said as he took the beer from Davin. "Mary?" he asked, and held out one for her.

"No, not right now, maybe later," she replied and then leaned back on the side of the boat and stared at the horizon. After staring for several minutes, she sat up and pointed, stuttering, "A boat, I see a boat!?"

After picking up the binoculars, Josh looked in the direction she was pointing, and saw what looked like a freighter on the horizon. "What the hell is he doing so far from the shipping lanes?"

"Whatever it is, it probably isn't good and we don't want to be picked up by them," Davin said, knowing full well that any ship that travelled off the designated shipping lane did not want to be seen. "Let's hope he doesn't see us. Even though we need to be rescued but being rescued by pirates or drug smugglers is not going to put us in a good position."

"Are you sure it is a pirate ship?" Mary asked.

"Not sure, but the flag he is flying shows she may be registered in Panama. Lower the canopy and stay low, let's not attract them," Josh watched as the ship slowly disappeared over the horizon.

"Keep an eye out, they may have friends," Josh stated. "We probably need to keep watch at night in case another one comes close."

"I will take first watch," Henry volunteered. "I will take a nap now so I will be rested. We probably should not transmit on the radio when I get it working, if there are those types of ships in the area, anyway."

"Good point, Henry. Sweet dreams, I will wake you after dark and will relieve you at midnight," Josh said. "No lights tonight, okay."

Chapter 30 This Is Not a Movie

"Miss Morgan, you know who I am. I am not here to harm you, but to trade information. You work for the CIA and we have been tracking you for the past year; and, well, I don't need to go into details, but I am ready to make a deal with you. It's a simple deal, one that your Director will greatly appreciate. But I need some information that you have or can get for me," Soon-Bok Kim stated after they took seats in the back of a small coffee shop in downtown Washington.

"Ok, go on. You have my attention, but I will not sell out my country," Joanne Morgan commented.

"Not to worry, I don't need any information about your country's secrets. What I need is the location of General Jin-Ho Shin. We know he was in Marseille, France; but lost him when he left when the local police were there. We know your CIA has been tracking him and that you know where he is. I need his location and I will give the name of the mole in your organization. The name I give you has been working for us for several years; our mole has provided a great number of secrets, but has recently become less helpful to us. To sweeten the deal, I will also tell you what was compromised. And yes, it will cause some problems within my government, but I can handle that. We need to get to General Jin-Ho Shin as quickly as possible. One other thing, the people that are tracking him need to stop. I was ordered to eliminate them if they get in the way, but really don't want to kill them. I will meet with Shin, and then your people can have him. But they need to let me enter his location without interference. If they interfere, I will have to stop them; and it will not be good for them if I have to."

"Interesting deal, Ms Kim, but I don't know where Shin is. If I did, I would tell you. Not even sure I can get the information you want but will try, if you allow me a couple of hours."

"You have two hours; meet me at the Watergate lobby. Come alone with the information, and I will hand over your mole and much more," Kim said and then indicated to her men that they were leaving.

"I will be there," Morgan stated as she watched Kim and her escorts leave the coffee shop.

Morgan stayed in the coffee shop and finished her latte. She then stood, and walked slowly toward the door in deep thought. She knew she had to go to the Director with this; she could not cover it up; she needed the information Kim had requested, and the only way was to talk to the Director. Uncovering the mole in the CIA was the top priority within the organization. This could be the break they needed to clean up the agency. It would take twenty minutes to get back to the campus. She thought about calling, but without a secure line she didn't want it to leak out that she was about to uncover the mole. The mole might be the one that answered the phone. She decided not to call, but to just show up and ask.

Twenty-five minutes later, she was walking through the front door of the agency building after parking in the visitor parking lot out front. After passing through the metal detector and showing her credentials to the guards, she was allowed to continue and keep her weapon. She took the first available elevator up to the second floor where Director Ashley Peterson's office was located. After she entered the office, she was confronted by Mrs. Helen French, Ashley's personal secretary and administrative assistant.

"Hello, Ms Morgan, Director Peterson is not in. She will be back in about an hour. Is there anything I can help you with?"

"No, I do need to see her as soon as possible. It is of extreme importance, can we contact her?" Morgan asked.

"If it is that important, I will try to contact her. Please take a seat and let me call her," Helen said and indicated the overstuffed black chair across the office. Joanne turned, sat and waited.

Five minutes later, Helen looked up from her phone and said, "Ms Morgan, I just spoke with the Director and explained to her that you needed to see her on an extremely urgent matter. She will be here in ten minutes. Would you like some coffee, tea or soda?"

"Some water would be nice, thank you."

Helen got up and walked over to a credenza and opened the left door exposing a small refrigerator. She removed a cold bottle of water and handed it to Joanne.

Eight minutes later, Ashley Peterson walked through the door and signaled for Joanne to follow, "Please close the door behind you, Joanne. What can I do for you?"

"When I left Walter Reed after seeing the doctor, I was picked up by Soon-Bok Kim," Joanne started to say but was stopped by Ashley.

"What about the President, first?" Ashley asked.

"He is fine, he was poisoned but they caught it in time to provide an antidote. You were correct in asking about the TOX screening."

"Good, now what is this thing with Kim, you know who she is; don't you?"

"Yes, I do and that is what worries me. She and three of her body guards picked me up. We went to a coffee shop about ten minutes from the hospital, and there she made a very strange offer which I think we need to accept," Morgan began, pausing for a second.

"An offer? What kind of offer does the Commander of the Korean Secret Police want to make?"

"She said she knows who our mole is, and will give him up along with everything he told them for the location of a General Jin-Ho Shin. She did not say why she wants him, but I suspect she is here to arrest him."

"Is that all she wants?"

"Yes, that for the mole," Joanne responded.

"How do we know she is not just giving a name of one of our people just to get Shin's location?"

"We don't, but she guarantees she will give us the right person."

"Okay, when do you meet her again to make the trade?" Ashley asked as she picked up her desk phone.

"In an hour, in the lobby of the Watergate."

"Gutsy, meeting there; but it's her call. I am sure she will have her protection team there. They can't be armed, but knowing Koreans that will not matter," Ashley said, dialed a number, and then held up her finger indicating for Joanne to be quiet and wait. Ashley turned slightly in her chair and spoke quietly into the handset.

"Okay, so we make the deal; and hopefully, she is not lying. I have the head of the operation coming up right now, and she can verify where Shin is right now."

Minutes later, there was a knock on the door. Ashley pushed a button on the side of her desk in the leg well which unlocked the door and in entered Elizabeth Grayson.

"Come in Liz, do you know Joanne Morgan?"

"No, pleasure Ms Morgan, may I call you Joanne?"

"Sure Liz," Joanne replied but a bit confused at the formality.

"Liz, we need an update on General Shin, his present location and activity. Can you provide that to us in the next few minutes?"

"Sure, he is in Cannes, France at a villa on the coast; I will get you the address. We have agents watching the house and they report in every half hour. Is there a problem, do we need to pull back?"

"No problem at the moment, but things are about to change and your people may have to move in quickly. Please inform them to be on their toes for the next forty-eight hours. But not to move in or do anything; stay in the shadows as it were."

"Okay, you can ask, but I can't answer right now. I don't have all the information I need to answer your question."

"I will be right back with the address, or can I just call down to ops to get it?" Liz asked.

"Sure use my phone," Ashley said and pointed to the phone on the credenza. Liz called down to her operations center and got the information needed, passed it to Ashley and Joanne, and then left the office. An hour later, Joanne was sitting in the lobby of the Watergate waiting for Soon-Bok Kim and her body guards. She did not have to wait long. Kim entered the lobby and walked directly to Joanne and sat down across from her. After a few tense moments without any talking, Kim opened her briefcase and pulled out a large manila envelope and laid it on the coffee table in front of her.

"That is everything I promised, the name and everything that was passed to us. You can do whatever you like with it and your mole. Have you got Shin's location for me?" Kim said pointing to an envelope.

"Yes," Joanne said and handed Kim a small envelope. "This is his current location and you must know we have a team watching him and his chalet. We will inform them of your arrival, and they will not bother you. If we don't let them know, they may stop you from interfering."

"Tell them I will arrive tomorrow and not to interfere. I have business with Shin and would prefer not to be bothered, thank you," she said and then stood and started for the door. She stopped a few feet away from Joanne and said, "Thank you, Ms Morgan, and one other thing, please don't enter my country again; if you do, I will have no choice but to arrest you for spying."

"Understood, thank you for the warning," Joanne agreed.

Twenty-four hours later

Soon-Bok Kim showed up at the Chalet of General Jin-Ho Shin at eleven-fifteen the next day, casually walked up to the front door, and rang the bell. Shin opened it himself and stood in shock as he looked at the Commander of the North Korean

171

Secret Police. He immediately knew he would not live much longer, and tried to slam the door on her. This action was met with resistance from her three body guards. They pushed open the door, closed it behind them, and locked it. What happened next was only speculation from Polson and his team outside. They saw Kim and two men enter the house; and ten minutes later, they heard, over the planted microphones, three muffled gun shots. Seconds later, they heard the roar of an engine and saw a boat racing away from the chalet.

CIA Headquarters

Ashley Peterson had the information about the mole, but was taking her time to investigate to ensure they would not arrest the wrong person. It would take a week of careful watching and setting a trap; but she already had it in motion, bringing in only four other agents to help with the trap.

Chapter 31 Return of the Nazis

Late the night before and early in the morning, one hundred ten large trucks and vans entered the city using different roads. The trucks and vans were disguised as *United Parcel Service* (*UPS*), *Federal Express*, and other locally operated delivery services. There were no semi-truck trailers, since they were not permitted within the city. This was because the roads were too narrow and the turns too sharp for such vehicles. Trucks no longer than twenty-eight feet were being used to carry the attackers.

Each vehicle stopped at a specific location within the city. Inside each vehicle were heavily armed Nazi soldiers about to strike terror within Washington D.C. Once each driver reached his or her designated position, a dozen soldiers dressed in civilian clothing exited their vehicle and started to move into their assigned positions. Each carried a small easily hidden machine gun, grenades, and eight fully loaded magazines. Since it was February and cold, their heavy coats provided the needed concealment. The rest remained in the trucks until ordered to proceed with their mission. Eighteen of the large moving vans parked within a block or two from the eighteen police precincts within the city. Approximately sixty soldiers were in each moving van. They were dressed in full combat gear and armed with light to heavy machine guns and Rocket Propelled Grenade (RPG) launchers.

At exactly seven in the morning, the attacks had started on Washington D.C. police officers and their precincts. The precincts were attacked with a combination of small arms and RPGs from multiple directions. They were coordinated attacks, all happening at exactly seven in the morning, to occur during the usual shift change when there were a lot of officers coming and going. The officers, identified by their uniforms, in patrol cars or walking a beat were just gunned down without warning. Overall, more than two thousand Metro police were killed and many more injured, effectively cutting the police protection for the city nearly down to zero.

Additionally, Fort Meade was attacked and almost overrun by the attacks. Fort Meade was well protected by the Army who were able to repel the attackers, but not without losses. The forces protecting CIA Headquarters were on alert as they are always and also repelled the attackers, losing five men during the attack. The building was hit by three RPGs and several people were killed. Major damage occurred to the second and third floors.

Both the CIA Headquarters and NSA at Fort Meade were immediately put on lock down and the guard forces were enhanced. Ashley Peterson was sitting in her office when the attacks started. She immediately reached for her weapon when an RPG slammed into the building four offices from hers. Ashley was knocked to the floor and struck her head on the desk on the way down. She lay unconscious on her office floor during the entire attack.

At the Capital building, the officers protecting the building and its occupants were not as lucky. As usual, there were only six officers on duty: four were on walking patrol and the other two were manning the door running the metal detector as people came and left the building. The attackers entered the building, approached the metal detector, immediately pulled their pistols, and shot the guards. At the same time, the four roving guards were gunned down. Once the six guards were down, the shooters started to shoot anyone they saw, killing twelve more. One of the attackers ran out to the flag pole, pulled down the American flag, and replaced it with the red flag with the Nazi swastika.

On Pennsylvania Avenue, a large force of attackers stormed the White House. They overtook the gate guard, and rammed a dump truck into the fence. It was Armageddon all over. Within minutes, the White House was breached and the attackers charged into the Oval Office only to find it empty. Vice President Bell, along with six Secret Service agents, had already taken the elevator down to the bunker where he had already been transferred by train to Mount Weather.

Chapter 32 Checking Out

"Doc, when can I get out of here?" President Mitchell asked when Doctor Dobrinski entered the President's private room.

"Not for a while, sir. We have to ensure your system is completely clear of the poison and that will take most of today to complete. If all is well, I will release you tonight."

"Sounds good to me, but another day of hospital food is going to put me back in the hospital," Mitchell said jokingly.

"The food here isn't bad; it hasn't killed anyone lately," Dobrinski replied as he scanned the charts and looked at the electronic equipment Mitchell was plugged into.
Suddenly, an alarm started to scream down the hall. Doctor Dobrinski stopped reading the chart and looked up and then ran out of the room and down the hall.

"What's going on?" he yelled at the nurse at the reception desk.

"There has been a bombing and we have injured coming in," she responded, and then picked up her remote and switched to the news channel on the television. What they saw was impossible to fathom, but the news cameraman was catching it live. The announcer broke in to report that the police stations in the city had been bombed, and reports were coming in that police stations around the city had been bombed with multiple deaths and hundreds injured.

"Stand by, more… wait a second. Military bases around Washington D.C. have been attacked by forces unknown and wait," the announcer stopped and then he yelled, "They are shooting at us!" "Let's get out of here!" he yelled at his driver, and the camera was still running as they ran for cover. Suddenly the filming stopped, and all they could hear were gun shots and explosions. She switched channels and they saw a helicopter flying low over a large red brick building and the caption said it was the National Security Agency located outside of Washington. The top floor was on fire and people were running out of the building. The helicopter turned and all they saw was the highway with a line of cars heading out of the city. Then it went blank and the announcer came on, "We are flying over to CIA Headquarters from where we have received reports that it has been attacked."

President Mitchell walked up behind Doctor Dobrinski and quietly said, "I am leaving, Doc. The country needs me, now."

"Nurse, will you call the White House and get the president's car and security. He is leaving," Dobrinski ordered.

"Thank you doc, I will get dressed," Mitchell said, realizing he was standing in the hall in his hospital gown. He turned and quickly walked back to his room. His guards followed him back to the room and assisted in getting the president ready to leave.

"Sir, I don't know what is going on, but until we do, I will not leave your side," the guard stated looking around the hospital for any threats.

"Thank you, Nate," Mitchell said and then turned on his TV.

"For those of you that have just tuned in, we are flying over Washington, at least until we are told to vacate the air. Fort Meade, home of the National Security Agency has been attacked. We are unsure of the number of dead, but the agency building is on fire. The base fire department is on the scene and handling the fire. We just flew over close to CIA Headquarters and we were escorted away by two Army attack helicopters. There is smoke coming from the building, but we could not tell how much damage has been done. Wait, we have just received word from flight control to return to the airport and land. All civilian flights have been cancelled until further notice. Wait, I am getting more information from our station; we have unverified reports that several members of Congress and the Senate have been killed and others injured in attacks. Additional information to follow as soon as we get it. That's all for now. I have been ordered to cease transmitting. Thank you."

"Hell, what is going on. I am out of the office for a few days and all hell breaks loose," Mitchell commented to Nate.

"I don't know, sir, but I know you will fix it," Nate commented.

"Let's go; the car should be here," Mitchell said just as Tony Sanford entered the door to his room.

"Tony what is going on?"

"Sir, Nazis. The city is under attack. We have ordered the military to respond in force; war has come home," Tony Sanford said quickly. "Let's go, I have a team downstairs to escort us back to the White House. Vice President Bell is there attempting to direct, but he is overwhelmed. He has never been in combat; he is an engineer."

Chapter 33 Detours

"Mr. President, we need to make a detour; the White House has been breached," Tony Sanford said to President Mitchell and then turned to the driver and said, "Point Alpha." The driver understood he needed to go immediately to the alternate secret entrance to the bunker. Only a few agents knew of this entrance. They were heading south on 16th Street when Sanford instructed the driver to go to Point Alpha. Turning right on Blagden Avenue NW, the driver accelerated and weaved through the traffic which luckily was light. He turned left on Beach Dr NW, and drove south again until he reached Tilden Street NW, and turned right. After pulling into the parking lot in front of Pierce Mill, Sanford, Mitchell and two Secret Service agents jumped out of the SUV and two more from the chase vehicle. All ran toward the Mill, entered, and walked pass the displays and through the door of the office located in the back of the mill. The secretary, sitting at her desk, immediately stood and greeted her new guests.

"This way gentlemen," she said and led them to what appeared to be a closet door. She pressed several buttons located behind a hidden panel; the door opened, and the agents, Sanford and President Mitchell entered. "Be safe, sir," she said as the door closed. Seconds later, the elevator descended to a platform that was seldom used except in emergencies such as this.

"Wow, how long has this entrance been here?" Mitchell asked.

"It was built when we did the refurbishment of the Mill. It was discovered that the Mill sat directly over the fast train we have between the White House and Mount Weather. It is only used in emergencies such as now."

"Where is Tara?"

"She is already in the bunker. We picked her up as soon as the attacks started to happen."

"Who are these guys?" Mitchell asked as they walked toward the train.

"Nazis"

"What?"

"Yes, Nazis, they have already run their flag up in front of the Capital Building and on the White House. Seems like they are working on taking over the country. What are you orders, sir?"

"Surround the city with the Army and National Guard. Take prisoners and take back the city without destroying it. Are these Nazis in some kind of uniform? If they are in uniform, attempt to arrest; if they resist, shoot to kill."

"Yes, some are. You got it sir, we are at war."

"Good, it is easier to tell who the bad guys are when they are in uniform. We are at an undeclared War!"

Chapter 34 Little Orange Rubber Boat

"Okay, Captain, where are we?" Davin asked after Blair had taken more sightings early in the evening of the third day. Food and water were getting low, morale was still high, but the chance of survival was also getting low. They were not as hopeful as they were when their plane went down. It had been three days since they decided to take a swim in the Atlantic Ocean.

"Well, not good; it could be my homemade sextant is not as accurate as I would like, but it looks like we have drifted about fifty miles. At this rate, we will be, well, out of food and water long before we see land," Blair reported, not speaking very loud because he did not want to alarm everyone on board. They had seen two other ships on the horizon in the past forty-eight hours, but they were too far away and there was no way they could be seen in their tiny orange rubber boat.

"Speak up, Captain. I couldn't hear you. What are you really trying to say?" Josh said a little louder than he normally spoke.

"Okay, I said we haven't drifted more than fifty miles, and to put it bluntly, we will be long dead before we reach land. Okay, satisfied?" Blair said getting a little testy.

"Yep, we have another day of food and water, five beers and a half bottle of Tequila. After that we are toast," Josh replied back.

"Well, Henry, any luck with those radios?" Davin asked.

"No, they are toast. Even with my advanced training, I can't fix those radios. If I had a complete lab and spare parts, maybe, but even that would be iffy," Henry replied, shaking his head. Everything he had tried proved to be futile in fixing one or both of the radios.

"Okay, I am not about to give up, yet. Although we are trained in survival and have been responsible with our food and water, we still are hundreds of miles from land or possible rescue. It is also possible they have called off the search and are not even looking for us," Josh commented.

"Have you noticed the clouds building to the east of us?" Mary said, pointing to the east.

"Yes, which means we may be in for a bit of a storm. It is not hurricane season so no worries about a hurricane, but storms out here can be a bit rough. I suggest that, in the next couple of hours, we secure anything that we don't want to lose overboard. And as the storm gets closer, we need to strap ourselves to the boat," Blair suggested looking grim.

"Agreed, Henry, is there any chance we could at least transmit on the emergency radio?" Josh asked.

"I tried everything I know to fix them, but the internals are fried," Henry answered tossing the radio to Josh, "Take a look yourself. Maybe you can find something I missed."

"I am no electronic technician, Davin, you take a look. You know more about these things than I do," Josh said and handed the radio to Davin.

"Okay, but I don't know that much more than you do."

Chapter 35 War Zone

Washington D.C. had become a war zone. The unarmed residents took up what they could to defend themselves. Some picked up weapons dropped by the gunned down police. Other residents, who did not abide by the law of no weapons to be held by civilians within the Metropolitan Washington District, unlocked their hidden safes and armed themselves. The residents that could meet with their neighbors formed resistance groups, similar to those formed in France during the Second World War. Many residents were able to evacuate the city, heading to anywhere that was safe. But many more were trapped; and although they were armed, they had no way of escape. They could communicate via cell phone and amateur radio with the world, but were still trapped.

The morning of day two of the occupation, large groups of Nazis in full uniform and heavily armed were seen patrolling the streets, and arresting or shooting any citizen that happened to have made the mistake of being on the streets. A curfew had been put in place; the efficiency of the Nazi group was extremely precise. Of the eight thousand Nazi soldiers that participated in the takeover, only sixty were killed and sixteen injured by return fire from the police or resistance from the citizens of Washington. The total citizens killed numbered in the hundreds and the Washington Metro police were in shambles; more than three quarters of the force was either killed or arrested and put in their own jails. The ones that were not joined up with the resistance groups to head up counter attacks against the Nazi invasion.

Posters were being placed all over the city, and local radio stations were broadcasting that the Third Reich had taken control of Washington D.C. and anyone that resisted would be arrested or shot. Makeshift concentration camps were being established around the city for those that did not abide with the new laws in place, not paying attention to the curfew or seen with a weapon. Even with the curfew and roving Nazi guards, many people were able to slip out of the city. As yet, there was no wall to climb; that was still to come. It would be Berlin all over again.

The United States Army and National Guard units had put up a solid parameter around the district, only letting out citizens that were running for their lives. It was a stand-off of epic proportion.

In command of the Army units was Major General Lester Pride, a Viet Nam, Desert Storm, Afghanistan veteran, highly decorated and very convinced that he could retake the city inside of three days; but until he received orders from the President, he just waited. And while waiting, he provided a blockade around the city.

As part of the takeover, Reagan International Airport Tower was overrun, and the Nazis had control of the airport. No aircraft departed or landed unless they said so. Twelve older C-123s and ten C-130s landed and unloaded more Nazi troops and heavy equipment, including missile launchers, APCs, several attack helicopters and assorted support equipment. Several more helicopters were able to slip under the U.S. Air Force cover that was put into the air quickly after the attacks started. The Nazis were planning a long visit to the city and brought the equipment and supplies to make sure of it. This army was well funded, well trained, and equipped.

Orders were given to the US pilots flying over the city that any aircraft that attempted to enter the airspace over Washington D.C. or attempted to land at Reagan International was to be considered hostile and shot down.

Two F-16 Fighting Falcons were circling over the outside of Washington when they got the order to fly over the White House and take pictures of any military visible. At fifteen thousand feet, both F-16s descended to five thousand and turned toward inner Washington.

"Wolfman, descending to five thousand. Stay close. We are cleared to fire if fired upon," Joker ordered as he pulled his power back a little to start his descent.

"Roger, Joker. All weapons hot; let's go take some pictures," Wolfman replied. The flight to the White House would only take a couple of minutes even at their reduced speed of about two hundred ten knots. Both were ready to go to combat power if threatened.

'*Target in sight, switching on cameras,*' Joker said to himself as he turned slightly to the left to line up on the White House and also be able to make a low pass over the mall. "Damn, do you see what I see Wolfman?"

"Yeah, can I shoot that thing down?"

"Only if they shoot at us; the new ROE applies here, Wolfman," Joker responded referring to the Rules of Engagement that had been put in place during Desert Storm and modified again during the Afghanistan war; and then to himself he said, *'We could lie and shoot that bloody Nazi flag down.'*

"Wow, and it only took two days to take us down." After pausing for a moment, he continued, "We have missile lock; let's get out of here… MISSILE LAUNCHED, MISSILE LAUNCHED!" Wolfman yelled over the radio. "We have missiles in the air," he reported to base.

"Dropping chaff and flares," Joker said as he went to full power afterburner and pulled hard back on his stick, "Going ballistic. Are you still with me Wolfman?"

"Banking right and climbing, still with…" his transmission was interrupted with an explosion. The missile on his tail exploded when it hit one of the flares he had dropped. "Sorry that was too close, I am still with you, Joker."

"Let's go light them up," Joker said as he turned his F-16 into a full afterburner dive back toward the mall and the missile launcher that had just fired on them. "Got a lock, one away!" And then he pulled up his F-16 and leveled at eight thousand feet with Wolfman close on his wing taking pictures. An award winning picture was number fifty-six in the sequence of photos.

"Great shot, Joker, scratch one missile launcher and a few Nazis," Wolfman reported. "I think we have enough for the brass; let's get out of here before they figure out where the launch button is again, on that other launcher."

"Roger that," Joker said and started a climb back to fifteen thousand feet and pulled back on his power below combat power.

Chapter 36 Presidential Nightmare

"Okay, bring me up to date. I know a group of Nazis have attacked and taken over the city. I know that Major General Pride is in command and has the city blockaded with troops from the 101st, 82nd and various National Guard units. He is a good man, but a little hot headed at times. I want to keep him on a short leash, understand, Tony," Mitchell said as he sat behind his desk in the underground Oval Office.

"All true, we just got a report that Pride ordered two F-16s to fly over and take pictures of the city, looking for gun emplacements, troops, anything military. While taking pictures, they were fired on by a surface to air missile. They were able to evade being hit; one F-16 sustained some damage when the missile hit one of the flares fired to divert the missile. Obviously it worked, but it was pretty close when it exploded. No injuries to either pilot; and they got some pretty good photos, including one when they were authorized to return fire and were able to destroy the launcher that had fired on them. They returned to base after taking the pictures and firing one missile to destroy the launcher. We will have copies of the photos in about an hour.

"Good, can you get Pride down here in the next few hours to discuss strategies? I want to be completely involved in the retaking of our city," Mitchell asked and paused to think for a moment, "What else do we know about these Nazis? Like how many are there of them, what are their capabilities, intentions?"

"Capabilities we are working on; intentions unknown except for what they already have done. How many, we are not sure, but initial estimates are that they have at least five to eight thousand troops, possibly more. The pictures will give us a good estimate of the equipment they have; but until we get someone on the inside, we may never know how many there are. They are flying in more troops and equipment to Reagan and then moving it into the city."

A light knock on the door interrupted their conversation, "Come in," Mitchell yelled to the unknown person on the other side.

"Good evening, Mr. President, Mr. Sanford," Ms Ashley Peterson said as she entered the office.

"Are you okay?" Mitchell asked seeing the bruise on her forehead and blood on her blouse.

"I am fine. When we were attacked, I was in my office and an RPG hit the building four offices down the hall, killed three and I was knocked to the floor. The blood isn't mine. I came here as soon as I made sure the injured were taken care of and the building secured. Our guard force has it locked down pretty tight. Pride also dispatched two platoons of infantry from the 82nd to assist. Fort Meade is also secure. On top of all this, we have another problem."

"What could top what is going on now? The city is under siege and effectively in enemy hands."

"Well, it is not worse than the city being in enemy hands?"

"It is not worse for us, but it is worse for three of my top operatives and two of my pilots and one airplane."

"What do you mean?"

"I don't want to trouble you with this, but I wanted to inform you that our Gulfstream has disappeared. They were on a Trans Atlantic flight when they disappeared. We dispatched S&R but no oil slick, wreckage or debris was located. It has been four days; and while we have expanded the search, we have reduced the number of search craft to three aircraft. They have not found anything. We feel they are all dead and will call off the search if nothing is found in the next forty-eight hours."

"Sorry to hear about your loss. Who are the agents?"

"Pierce and Randal, Captain Blair, Henry Siegel, and Mary Becks were all on board, they were following Hans Bormann," Peterson reported.

"Damn," Tony said.

"There is more. We received a report from one of our field ops that the body of Bormann has been found in an abandoned warehouse about one hundred miles south of Berlin."

"Wasn't he our connection to this Nazi thing?" Mitchell asked.

"Yes, we had placed a tracker chip in him when we had him in Gitmo. We allowed him to escape, and Pierce and Randal were following him. They left Bermuda bound for Madrid. When Bormann's tracker showed his vital signs as deceased, we had our op in Berlin check it out. We did not inform him how we knew where he was, just told him we got a tip. The body had one bullet hole in his head, right between his eyes, nine millimeter."

"Okay, again sorry for the loss; they were both good men. I never met Blair, Siegel and Becks, but feel for their loss also. Next of kin notified yet?" Mitchell said. He paused for a moment to take in everything he had heard, and then continued, "Have you got anything about our invaders?" Mitchell asked.

"Yes I do. I am going to meet with Ms Pierce and Randal right after this meeting; I also have two agents going over to the pilot, copilot and our agent on board families," Peterson said, and then briefed him on everything they had gathered on Bormann and who she thought was behind the invasion.

"Who is behind this?" Mitchell asked cutting her short.

"Gregory Dietrich, he is a German national, grandson to a Nazi that was known as Sepp. Dietrich is a known Nazi organizer and we have been watching him for a long time. Can't pin anything on him, but all indications are that he is responsible for this."

"Gregory Dietrich, where have I heard that name before?"

"Michelle Dietrich is an up and coming actress; she just arrived in Hollywood for an audition for a movie. She was also on that American Airlines flight that had the virus onboard. She may have been a carrier, but we can't prove it; so we had her released and she flew on to Los Angeles where she said she had a screen test," Ashley replied, "We have been watching her also, but she does not seem to be anymore than Gregory's sister. He probably sent her to Hollywood to make sure she was safely away from harm and possibly did not know she was a carrier of a deadly virus. We can have the FBI pick her up and hold her for questioning."

"Make it so," Mitchell ordered and then turned to Tony Sanford, "With the city under Nazi control, we don't have too many options do we?"

"Yes, and no, when Pride gets here I have a few ideas that may help," Sanford said just as the phone on the President's desk started to ring.

"This is Mitchell," he said as he picked up the phone, "Good send him in." After he hung up the phone, he announced, "Pride is here."

"Mr. President, pleasure to finally meet you. Before we talk you need to know that a private corporate style jet just landed at Reagan. Not sure who was on it, but the pilot was able to slip past our blockade and land. He came in under our radar and did some pretty fancy flying to avoid our guys."

"That may be our Nazi leader coming to claim his domain. This may just be to our advantage," Mitchell commented. "Please have a seat; we have a lot to discuss."
An hour after finishing the briefing with the President, Ashley Peterson was sitting across from Stephanie Randal and Connie Pierce in Connie's living room.

"Ladies, I have some bad news and wanted to tell you myself," Peterson started once they were all seated.

"What is it, Ashley?" Connie asked.

"Davin and Josh's plane is four days overdue in Madrid, Spain. Now before you get yourself worked up, we have ordered Air Sea Search and Rescue to locate them. Could be anything: from failure to close the flight plan, to diverting the flight to another airport. We are doing everything we can to locate them as quickly as possible."

"There is a lot of ocean out there, they could, ahh, have crashed," Connie said almost in tears. "

"We don't know, but are looking," Ashley said and the rest of the conversation centered on what could be done to locate the missing plane.

Chapter 37 Day Two of the Occupation

After moving into the city using moving vans, *UPS* and *FedEx* delivery trucks, the Nazis immediately eliminated as many of the Metro Police and any resistance they came upon as they moved deeper into the city and established a heavily defended perimeter around the Federal Corridor including the museums, treasury, and all the federal buildings within the city. The northern border ran along K Street, to the south along the 395, west to the Potomac, and east to 6th Street NE completely surrounding the Capitol building, White House, and all the monuments. They had enough men and material to secure the area and planned on not getting overrun.

The Nazis placed their heavy machine guns in strategic places around the city; and with delivery trucks, blocked every road, alley, and walkway into the area. A few old Panzer tanks and Soviet T-34s were also brought in and placed in defensive positions near the White House. They were prepared for all sorts of American attacks including tanks.

Over in the White House, Gregory Dietrich who had arrived on a private corporate jet a few hours earlier and was now sitting in the Oval Office smoking one of the President's cigars, was thinking that he had just pulled off the biggest and best attack in history. He and his men took control of the capital of the United States. He was in charge and his plan had come together with few losses. But he knew he would not be here long, just long enough to find the hidden passage to the bunker, which he knew was somewhere in this building.

"General, we have teams looking all over this building for that secret entrance to the bunker. Are you sure they have a secret entrance?" his lieutenant asked as he walked into the Oval Office. "We have found a staircase going down, but it was to several offices only and what looks like a war room. There were a couple of guards; we have them locked up."

"He has to have an escape route somewhere in this building and we need to find it. Finding it will allow us to escape into his deepest and darkest secret domain. Keep looking, it is here," Dietrich said.

"Yes sir," the lieutenant said and left the room smartly.

They had controlled the city for the past forty-eight hours, and so far, there had not been much activity in the way of resistance or counter attacks. He knew deep in his heart that he did not have much time. The Americans would mount a counter attack and quickly wipe out most of his forces. He knew their strength and that he would not win this war. But that was not his plan; his plan was to prove to the Americans that they were vulnerable and that even a small force of fifteen thousand soldiers could take their city quickly and with minimal losses. Well, minimal losses on his side, many losses to the American side. His troops had killed or wounded seventy-five percent of the police and armed resistance they encountered when they had started.

"Sir, we are getting reports from the outer perimeter that the Americans are provoking them, taking shots when they see a target. We have loss reports of twenty confirmed dead and twelve wounded. Their snipers are picking off our men when they become exposed," a Sergeant reported as he entered the Oval Office.

"Are we getting any of them?"

"No sir, they are using snipers and keeping their distance and remaining under cover."

"Tell our men to keep their head down or they could lose it. I expect they will mount a full assault sometime in the next twenty-four hours. Alert the men," Dietrich ordered. "Get Lieutenant Ritzel for me; immediately."

"Yes sir," the sergeant said, saluted and did a precision about face and exited the office.

"General Dietrich, Lieutenant Ritzel reporting as ordered, sir," Ritzel said standing in front of the desk at attention.

"Stand at ease, Lieutenant. Please take a seat; we need to talk," Dietrich said quietly, "But please close and lock the door before you sit."

"Yes, sir."

"You and several of my other best lieutenants helped plan this operation; and now that we are here, we have to prepare for the upcoming attack from the Americans, and I need your input. You have proven to me that you are my best tactician. We need a plan in case we can't find the bunker."

"Thank you, sir, but if that secret entrance is in this building we will find it," Ritzel commented and then continued, "But I think that we take the command staff out the back since we still have control of the land all the way to the Potomac. We move out within the hour, basically leave so we can fight another day."

"Right, not sure if I like that, but, I believe, that may be our best bet. However, I am not yet ready to vacant the most powerful country's office. But you are right, we need to leave

203

and soon. Inform the commanders and their teams that we move out in five hours; we will meet on the back lawn. It will be dark. Now move," Dietrich ordered and then waited as he heard a knock on the door. "Wait; that may be the information we need." After walking over to the door, Dietrich unlocked it, and opened the door where he was greeted by Lieutenant Nicklas.

"Sir we found the entrance; it is just down the hall. We haven't gotten it open yet, but will shortly," Nicklas reported.

"That is good; show me. Come, Ritzel, you need to see this too," Dietrich ordered.

Minutes later, they were standing in front of the hidden elevator. The wall was opened exposing the door to the elevator. Three soldiers were working on the control panel attempting to open the door, but not having much success.

"The security system has multiple access requirements. This is a retina scanner," the soldier said as he pointed to the eye level scanner and then to the key pad. "This is the key pad which requires a six digit code to access, and besides, it is a card scanner. Any combination of the three keys are required to open the doors; in other words, it may require only two of the three control keys or may require all three."

"Can you crack it?" Dietrich asked looking at the key pad.

"It will take time, but yes, I can crack it," the soldier said, "I used to build the German version of these things back in Germany."

"Good, you have three hours; if we can't crack it, we need to vacate. We leave in five hours."

Chapter 38 Adrift and Alone

Day four came with a bang. The storm had caused the seas to kick up and the swells were now eight to ten feet. They had pulled the top completely over the raft to keep the rain out and them inside. But the ride could be equated to an 'E' ride of the old days at Disney World where rides were rated 'A' to 'E'. The 'E' ride was the scariest and most active in movement and thrills. Each of the riders clung to their side of the raft for dear life.

As the storm intensified, the occupants were being thrown from side to side; and several times, the raft became airborne and flipped over, only to right itself on the next swell. The rain came down in buckets, sounding as if they were inside a steal drum. The hours passed slowly as the storm ran its course. Eventually it started to subside and the rain slowed to a gentle beat.

"Wow, I haven't been on a ride this intense since Space Mountain opened at Disney World and that was only for a few minutes. How long has this storm been pounding us?" Davin commented and asked.

"Four and half hours, is everyone okay?" Josh answered.

"I am fine," Mary replied, "But could use some fresh air."

"Okay over here," Blair answered reaching up to unfasten the catch that held the top together.

"Sorry about the mess, I will clean it up. First time I have ever been sick on a plane or boat," Henry commented.

"A little bruised, but fine otherwise; thanks for asking," Davin replied. "So, do you think that storm blew us anywhere near land or a ship?"

"We shall see," Blair said as he pushed the top down to expose the sun just setting to the west. "Sun is going down and if the clouds clear, I should be able to get a good sighting and see where we are."

"What the hell?" Josh commented looking up at the hull of a rusty freighter that was not more than twenty feet from their tiny little orange boat. "Ahoy up there!" he yelled and got no answer after several tries.

"I don't hear any engine running," Blair commented. "She may be adrift like we are."

"There is a ladder hanging over there; let's grab it and let ourselves on board," Davin said, not hearing anything from the freighter.

With a bit of difficulty, they were able to get their little boat over to the ladder and tie up. Josh pulled out his weapon and checked for a round in the chamber.

"Do you think you will need that?" Henry asked.

"Don't know, just want to be careful. Davin, Mary have you got yours ready?" he asked as he reached up and started to climb the rope ladder after getting a nod from both of them. "Watch my back and come up as quickly as possible."

"Roger that, old man," Davin replied as he reached for the ladder to steady it as Josh climbed. Upon reaching the top, he glanced back down to his friends and said to himself, *"Holy shit, looks like a war zone."*

"What do you see?" Davin asked from half way up the ladder, "The rest of you come on up as quickly as possible."

"War zone, hurry," Josh said as he took up a defensive posture, with his weapon at the ready position, and looked around at the four bodies lying on the deck. The deck was wet from the rain, but there were dark stains under and around each body. Davin climbed over the rail and stepped to the right of Josh and both waited for Mary, Blair and Henry to join them.

"Looks like a hijacking gone bad," Davin commented and walked over to the closest body. Upon rolling him over, he saw

208

multiple bullet holes in the victim. "Yeah, hijacking gone bad for sure."

"Okay, Mary, Henry you are with me; Davin and Blair go forward and see what you can find. We will head to the bridge. Blair, take this," Josh said after checking the Glock Model 30 he saw lying on the deck near one of the victims. It was loaded with two rounds missing from the clip.

Davin picked up another pistol; a Berretta 9 mm with six rounds fired, and handed it to Henry. "You know how to use this?"

"For sure, eight years in the Army, carried one of these in Desert Storm," Henry replied as Davin handed him an extra magazine he found on the body. After splitting up, each group headed in a different direction.

"Meet on the bridge in thirty minutes; fire a single shot if you run into trouble. Multiple shots if your need help right away," Josh ordered as he, Henry and Mary headed off toward the stern.

Thirty minutes later, an almost complete survey of the ship resulted in finding three more bodies in the bow area and four more as Josh and Mary approached the bridge. Upon entering the bridge, they found the captain in a pool of blood with a military issued M-16 in his hands. The magazine was empty and brass casings were all over the bridge; it was obvious that he went down fighting. Major damage to the bridge had occurred when the grenade, that had killed him, exploded.

"Henry, check the radio room," Josh ordered pointing toward the open door at the back of the bridge.

"Josh, we found several more dead, and collected the weapons; it looks like there was a major battle here and the crew lost. Some of the ones we saw did not look like crew, but attackers. For some reason, the attackers left in a hurry either before or after they got what they wanted," Davin said as he and Blair entered the bridge laying the weapons on the control panel.

"Ship has a little list to starboard, but not enough to be dangerous. Engines are cold, and no one is alive down there," Blair added. "And one life boat is missing."

"Radios are dead too; they have been shot to hell, literally," Henry reported when he arrived back at the bridge.

"Okay, at least we are dry, for now anyway. Let's see if we can get this tub moving in the right direction. Does anyone here know anything about starting those engines down there?" Josh asked.

"Well, I guess that would be me. Part of becoming a pilot meant we had to understand the workings of engines, so Henry and I will go down and see what we can do with them," Blair said and started for the door.

"Keep your eyes and ears open; there still could be others on board," Davin commented.

"Roger that," Blair replied.

Chapter 39 America Rises

"General Pride, you are an aggressive leader, and I know you have a plan in your mind to remove the Nazi intruders from our city," Mitchell stated as he started the meeting as soon as General Pride took a seat across from President Mitchell. "So, let's go to the war room where we have a map of the city and aerial photos of troops, gun emplacements and, well, all the information that you need to lay out your plan."

"Sir, I must say you do get right to the point. I like that," General Pride replied.

"Let's go," Mitchell said and stood and walked to the door. Minutes later, they were standing in the War Room surrounded by photos, maps, and six intelligence operations members.

"Okay, sir. Let me look this over for a couple of minutes; you have some information I had not received yet," Pride stated as he started to scan each photo, and communication transcript. He then watched as an overlay was placed on top of the map of Washington. The overlay showed all known locations of troops, missile emplacements, and aircraft.

"Sir, please take a look at the big screen," an Intel Op said and pointed to the one hundred two inch projection on the south wall. Almost as if by magic, the screen came alive with a map of the White House, and Capital Mall which was surrounded by the museums. All over the screen were little red dots that were moving slowly around, each dot representing a person. After careful studying of the movements of each dot, it became easier to determine who was a Nazi, resistance fighter, or civilian, just hiding and trying to be safe.

"I'm not going to ask, but, damn, we had a similar system during Desert Storm. It was not this good," Pride stated and then asked, "Can we move it around the city?"

"Yes, the city is roughly a ten by ten mile oblique grid. We have broken the city down into five zones numbered one to five, starting in the northwest corner; you just ask for the area and we will bring it up. Zone One is Arlington, Falls Church, and areas west of the Potomac River. They are not concentrated there at all. Their forces are all on the east side of the Potomac River. The White House, Capital and mall is Zone Five which overlaps the other four zones. The rest of the city is divided into four grids with overlapping edges. Zone Three goes down to Alexandria and most of the bay area, in which we have not seen any troops.

As I said, they are on the east side of the Potomac. We will be concentrating on Zones Two, Four and Five. We can zoom into any area for a better view."

"Can we see the entire city in one shot?"

"Yes, but with the size of our screen, we will lose some of the clarity," the operator stated.

"May we see it? And project each zone on different monitors around the room," Pride asked as he looked around the room and saw three more eighty-inch monitors.

"Sure, but it will take a while to get the other monitors set up. Can you give me an hour or two, sir?" the operator said with a smile.

"Take three, label each monitor with the zone it will project and keep the White House on the biggest monitor."

"Yes, sir," he said and then immediately turned and walked over to his team and issued orders. They left the war room to retrieve the additional monitors and other equipment to complete the modifications to the room.

President Mitchell looked over at Pride and smiled, "General your reputation said you were good, now I know it; let's step out and get a coffee while these people get the war room redone for us."

Mitchell, Pride and Sanford walked out and down the hall to the café which served this end of the bunker. After ordering coffee and a light snack, they took a table in the corner. The café at this hour was not busy so they could talk freely. The discussion ranged from the weather to possible scenarios to retake the city. Two hours later, the lead INTEL operative walked into the café and said, "Excuse me sirs, we are ready."

"Thank you, we will be right there," Mitchell said and then stood, "Let's go take our city back, gentlemen." The technician turned and walked swiftly back to the War Room. As they walked into the now dimly lit War Room, they saw the complete system lining up the walls. Each monitor showed a different zone of the city with the largest monitor showing the Capital, White House and Smithsonian complex along with surrounding government buildings. Each view covered approximately a five mile square of the city with overlapping edges.

"This is perfect; now we can take back our city, Mr. President. I have enough troops and equipment to move into the city from all sides. We also have been in contact with resistance cells throughout the city. They have been providing vital information as to troop movement and equipment placement ever since the first attack. Some of the resistance groups are being led by retired military, police officers that have been able to evade capture, and some by just good old civilians that are tired of being walked on; some may call them rednecks, I call them Americans," Pride commented as they walked into the room.

Chapter 40 Deadly Cargo

"Mary, you stay on the bridge and keep an eye out. Lock the doors, if they will lock, and keep your weapon close. Davin and I are going to cruise the ship and see what we can find and possibly learn why this tub is drifting alone," Josh ordered as he headed toward the bridge door.

"No problem, too bad we don't have radios," she commented, just wishing.

"See if you can get the onboard intercom working," Davin said as a joke, as he and Josh exited the bridge. Searching the bridge tower only took a few minutes and they found nothing out of the ordinary, except the cabins had been searched by someone looking for something. Working their way down into the hull of the ship, they checked the crew's quarters, galley, and then started into the cargo holds. The first hold was full of grain; the second hold was empty, except for about a foot of water. As they moved forward, they could hear the creaks and groans of the old ship.

"What do you think, Josh?" Davin asked.

"Well, not sure, this ship should be cut up and made into beer cans," Josh replied as they entered the next cargo bay.

"Wow, the mother lode! Davin, old buddy, we need to get some of this on ice," Josh exclaimed as he and Davin entered the bay and saw pallets of beer, vodka, tequila, wine and all sorts of other adult beverages. "Well we may not be moving very fast, but at least we will enjoy the cruise."

"We can come back for some of this; maybe there are some cold ones in the galley already. Let's finish checking out this tub; I am getting hungry," Davin said as they walked among the cases of liquid.

"Okay, I agree. Been a while since our last MRE," Josh said and headed for the next cargo bay.

"What's that?" Davin said pointing to the corner of the cargo bay.

"Don't know, looks like a large crate marked, this end up. Hell I don't know!" Josh exclaimed and walked over to the large crate. "Look it's open; what do you suppose was in it?"

"Do I look like a crate expert? But it looks like it may have been what our hijackers were after. The foot print in the bottom of the case shows it was on a tripod and was heavy," Davin said and kneeled down and picked up a sheet of 8x11 paper. "Look at this; it says here that the item in the crate was a vehicle mounted missile launcher. It looks like it housed a

Hellfire/DARG pedestal launcher. It is one of the newest systems that can be mounted on the back of a Humvee, pickup truck or even on a helicopter. Very deadly and extremely accurate, can use the Unguided Hydr-70 and the Guided DAGR missile which will lock on after launch which is laser guided."

"Hellfire, I saw a demo of that a few years ago. Very nasty little beastie. Wonder how many they got off this tub?" Josh commented.

"Let's see if there are any other empty crates; look, there seems to be room in this bay for at least a half dozen or more," Davin pointed out as he looked around the cargo bay.

"They must have had a larger boat to off load those onto," Josh said and started for the next bay again.

"Okay, let's move on, my stomach is making nasty sounds again," Davin reported and then opened the door to the next cargo bay. "Is this for real?"

"Yeah, I would say that is for real," Josh replied back as they both looked at the fully armed US Army Blackhawk helicopter. "I can truly say that they will be back for this. And we need to be ready when they do."

"No, we need to fly this bird off of this tub and go to the nearest land and call the Coast Guard. Whoever these people are, they are well funded and will want this bird."

"Let's finish this search and get back up to the bridge. This is getting a little weirder the further we go into this ship," Josh said and opened the door to the next bay. They found nothing too scary in the last bay, just a bunch of crates marked as Israel Weapons, Military Property. There was enough in the bay to support a brigade for weeks. There were crates of rifles, RPGs, handguns, and ammunition. "Let's get back to the bridge; I have a very bad feeling about all of this."

Minutes later, they were back on the bridge along with Blair and Henry.

"We have a real problem here, Captain; there is a Blackhawk in the number three cargo bay. And there are several crates with Hellfire/DARG missile launchers in them and a couple of them are missing. They may be coming back to get the rest or to drive this tub to wherever they need to go. If I were a betting man, which I am, I would bet they are coming back to take over this tub and deliver the cargo to their own base," Josh said and then took a seat in the corner of the bridge.

"I have to agree, Josh. What do you think we should do? They were probably here a while ago and removed the launcher and killed the crew. They must have another ship close by or we are closer to land than we thought," Davin replied and then looked at Captain Blair and Henry. "What are your thoughts, Captain?"

"Well, it was dark when we went down, and our instruments were not reporting that we were close to land; but then again, we floated and went through that storm, so our exact location is questionable at best. I tried to triangulate where we are right now with the primitive system they have on board. The GPS and other navigation equipment on board are non-functional. The pirates, terrorists or whoever boarded this boat and killed the crew and took that missile launcher also made sure the NAV gear and GPS were put out of commission. My best guess is that we are about two hundred fifty to three hundred miles off the coast of Africa, exactly which country is questionable. But we are no more than three hundred miles off the coast."

"How can you be so sure we are no more than three hundred miles off the coast?" Josh asked.

"I'm not. SWAG, my best Scientific Wise Ass Guess," Blair replied with a smile.

"That's what I thought, but I rely on your SWAG. We are no more than three hundred miles off the coast, but not in any shipping lanes, somewhere where the bad guys can work without being spotted or bothered. The satellites probably don't even fly over this part of the ocean," Josh agreed.

"Okay, so we are still a long way from being rescued on a ship loaded with military cargo that may be used against our troops or worst, against civilians within our country. We may have to sink this boat to keep those weapons from being used," Josh said.

"Sink it. If we sink it, where will we go?" Mary jumped in after listening intently to the conversation.

"Yeah, sink it and we will either fly off this tub or go down with her," Davin stated confidently.

"Okay, then we need to get that bird in the air," Mary stated, "I don't want to go swimming with the sharks again, once this week is enough. Besides, I don't have another change of clothing," she said laughing.

Chapter 41 Resistance Is Not Futile

After a couple of hours of scanning the monitors and determining where the Nazis and their fortifications were located with the help of the intelligence analysts, General Pride came up with a game plan that would cause the least amount of damage to the city, yet bring control back to the American people. But there were some if's that were not known to him or the team that assisted.

"Can you get President Mitchell and the Vice President in here?" General Pride asked as he continued to study the monitors.

"Yes, sir," the senior secret service agent replied and then stepped over to a phone and dialed a number. The agent spoke quietly for a moment and then hung up the handset. "They will be down in a few minutes, sir."

"Thank you."

Minutes later, the door opened and in walked President Mitchell, Vice President Bell, National Security Advisor Tony Sanford and two secret service agents. "Are you ready, General?" Mitchell asked.

"Yes, and no, sir. But I believe we have a workable plan. Please have a seat and I will explain," Pride started and then paused until everyone was comfortably seated. "I have been communicating with my senior advisors that are stationed around the city. And with their assistance, along with the information I have at my fingertips, we are ready to start a counter attack. Presently I have twenty thousand troops stationed around the city with everything from small arms to heavy weapons. We don't want to use the heavy weapons unless we really need to. So, I have had my commanders get in touch with the resistance located within the city. They are prepared to provide assistance in the form of distractions when we start our move into the city. The commanders of Zones One and Three also have amphibious assault teams which we will use to cross the Potomac during our retaking of the city. I am proposing we start our move from all sides at once, say at eight in the morning. They will expect us to do this. These people are not stupid, they planned a coordinated attack that crippled our police force immediately and blockaded themselves in our city. They did this quickly and without loss of much human life, on their side anyway."

"So your proposal is to do the same?" Mitchell asked.

"Yes, but unlike our Nazi attackers, we know where everyone of their troops are positioned and can communicate that to our forces to eliminate or capture them quickly. We also know where their heavy equipment is and we will take that out with our own missiles, either fired from helicopters, fighter jets or our little secret shoulder fired tank killers."

"So far, it sounds good," Mitchell replied. "Go on."

"Zones Three and Four will start moving into the city in the morning. We move in toward the known positions with our tanks; but at the same time, while they are concentrating on defending against our tanks, we will flank them and take them down. Movement through the city will be slow and dangerous; but by knowing where they are, we can take them down with minimal loss of life on both sides."

"Okay, Pride you don't need to go into anymore details; you have what sounds like a good plan, make it happen," Mitchell said quietly. "Can you do it tomorrow?"

"Yes, sir," Pride said and then turned to his team, "We have work to do." Pride then walked over to the encryption equipment and radio on the side table, switched it on and after a few seconds, he depressed the talk button and said, "Commanders we have a go for launch. Zero eight is launch time, we will send you the coordinates of all enemy locations in your sector between now and two hours prior to launch. And provide updates as required. Keep me posted as to all incursions and movement. Communicate with resistance as needed for assistance in movement. In sequence, respond with affirmative if you understand your orders."

"Zone One, confirmed"

"Zone Two, confirmed."

"Zone Three, confirmed."

"Zone Four, confirmed. We have movement, cancel report, we have evacuees coming out."

"Zone Four, defend your positions," Pride ordered and then looked at the President and said, "Zone Five is our objective. Since Zone Five is the most important, we want to push them out of there as quickly as possible; coming in across the river may be dangerous, but if we move troops tonight to strategic positions along the coast line, we will be sure they can operate."

"We are ready, sir. Give the word," Pride said to the President.

"Make it happen," President Mitchell ordered.

Chapter 42 The Beginning of the End

It was a cold, moonless night over Washington D.C.; the only movement was the one hundred Zodiac Milpro FC-530 Tactical operations inflatable boats, each carrying twelve heavily armed Marines. They were assigned to retake Reagan International Airport. Once they established positive control, they would cross the river and secure the southern boundary of the city. Under the command of Viet Nam and Desert Storm veteran Colonel Max Griffin, aka Mad Max, they were well trained and ready for a fight; most had recently returned from the Middle East where they had fought an enemy that had no respect for life.

Griffin never commanded from the rear, but always led the attack; he was first in the battle zone and the last to leave. He was like General Custer, but with one thing that Custer never had, superior firepower and hi-tech equipment allowing him to know exactly what he was up against. His men were briefed and knew their mission. Each member of the force had encrypted radios to communicate, if necessary, but would maintain radio silence unless they needed support to keep from being overrun or killed. Colonel Griffin was responsible for Zone Four, retaking of Reagan International Airport, and then back across the river to support the 82nd Airborne in their initial assault.

Knowing where the enemy had set up their machine guns and missile batteries should make their job easy, but even with the best laid plans, once the shooting started all plans go down the tubes.

Making their way across the Potomac was the easy part; each boat made shore and unloaded quickly without being seen. The teams spread out and took up defensive positions as ordered. Team Twenty-one was personally led by Colonel Griffin. "Hawkeye, Big Dog, Banzi, Riddler, we are moving closer. Cover our flanks," Griffin ordered at five in the morning, indicating Teams Nineteen, Twenty, Twenty-two, and Twenty-three respectively; as he signaled to his team to slowly move forward crossing West Bank Park. "Big Dog, Riddler, move in and secure your areas. All other teams maintain position."

"Home Base, Blackfish Alpha," Griffin, in charge of Team Twenty-one, said over his radio.

"Go ahead alpha," the operator replied.

"Update on enemy positions," he asked the operator.

"Roger, stand by," the operator said and then tapped a few keys on his computer, "You should see them on your monitor."

"Got them, this live?" Griffin asked, already knowing it was.

"Affirmative, I will keep the feed up until you say you are clear."

"Roger, thanks," Griffin said and then switched his radio to his field commanders, issued orders and said, "Execute when ready."

The taking of the airport was not an easy task; the Nazi teams had heavy weapons and were not afraid to use them. Hawkeye, Team Nineteen, under the command of Captain Roy Barrett, engaged the enemy as they moved toward the terminal. They started taking fire from several machine emplacements; three soldiers were wounded including Captain Barrett. After taking cover, they returned fire, but were not making a dent in the defenses. Captain Barrett pressed his transmit button and spoke quietly between the pain of his wounds, "Blackfish, this is Hawkeye, where is our air support?"

"Hawkeye, on the way, keep your heads down," Griffin replied.

Hawkeye had asked too soon, eighteen Apache helicopters popped up from the Potomac side and started to fire missiles into the parked Nazi aircraft and armed positions scattered around the airport. Within minutes, all the machine gun positions were smoking ruins; all but two of the Nazi aircraft were burning holes in the ground. The attacking teams moved in and took about an hour to eliminate the remaining Nazi terrorists.

"Blackfish, we have the terminal under control," Captain Barrett reported.

"Casualty report," Griffin requested. "All teams, clear all buildings and report when complete."

"Six dead, eight wounded," Barrett reported, not mentioning that he was one of the wounded.

"Roger. Keep it secure, and make sure you get that wound taken care of. Medi-vac is on the way," Griffin ordered, smiling at the courage of Barrett, continuing to fight even though he was wounded, and switched his radio to contact his other teams. "Hawkeye, Mustang and Rabbit fall back to the boats; we have objective two to handle. Let's go take back our capital," He ordered Teams Nineteen, Seven, and Eight to remain at the airport to maintain security.

Colonel Griffin took the balance of his Zone Four team across the Potomac and started up toward the Lincoln Memorial. They were spread out all along the coast; and once landed, they quickly took up defensive positions and linked up with elements from the 82nd Infantry Division. Griffin scanned his pad for position updates of both the enemy and his own forces. The technology they were using was the latest in combat equipment. The pad linked to a computer network that tracked movement via satellites using infrared imaging. Zone Four was the largest of the five zones but was mostly water. It also was the quickest way to the White House; the Nazis were entrenched around the Federal buildings and museums. The Nazis had established a stronghold in the southern half of Zone Five with heavy machine guns and several older model Soviet tanks positioned around the White House.

Griffin was unable to tell the difference between hostiles and civilians on his pad; but using a little deductive reasoning, he was able to determine that most of the civilians were being held captive inside the buildings, whereas the hostiles were on the corners and other strategic locations to defend themselves from an overpowering force about to retake the city.

Colonel Griffin and his team ducked behind the Viet Nam wall for cover. His eyes briefly scanned the wall where he saw some of the names and recalled the faces of the men he served with in Viet Nam. Some had come home walking, and some had not. He remembered all of them; they were his first team. Now, he had another team to bring home, and he was determined to make sure he brought them home. Quickly, he moved his team away from the wall; he did not want it to be damaged. Too much of the city had already been damaged by these terrorists; and he did not want any more damage, except to the terrorists themselves.

Moving under the cover of darkness, Griffin's team moved closer to the White House, and had not yet run into any resistance; it was only a matter of time. When they stopped on the edge of the Lincoln Memorial Reflecting Pool, his men laid down and scanned the area; using night vision goggles, they were able to see the machine gun emplacements on the other side of the pool. Seconds later, Griffin's headset clicked. He slid back behind one of the monuments on the edge of the pool, clicked and spoke. "Blackfish Alpha, go," Griffin said quietly into his headset.

"Home Base has a request," was the reply.

'Holy crap, what now?' Griffin said to himself and then into the headset, "What is the request?"

"The boss wants to be there when you take the house. He is on his way over; maintain your position until he arrives. He knows where you are," the order came across crisp and clean.

"We will comply," Griffin said quietly and then turned to his men and signaled them to maintain their position until the boss arrived; and then to himself he said, 'Why now? We are in a battle to take the city, and he wants to be in the middle.'

"Chevy and Cowboy, sit rep?" Griffin asked over the radio to Teams One and Eighteen.

"Chevy, in position. Other teams moving ahead, minimal casualties; lots of prisoners. Linked with Army units and holding ground," Chevy leader replied. Griffin could hear heavy machine gun fire in the background and only smiled. He was pleased; so far, the plan had gone as predicted. With the constant updates from General Pride's team on the location of the enemy and the assistance provided by the American resistance fighters, the takeover was moving along well. But, now, he had to put his team on hold until the General arrived. Twenty minutes later, Griffin's radio spoke again.

"Blackfish, Thor moving up behind you, don't shoot me." Thor, aka General Pride, commander of the operations was accompanied by a small team of Special Forces soldiers. Within minutes, Pride was lying beside Griffin with his team spread out behind them and asked, "What's the status?"

"We have taken all the enemy positions south of the Lincoln Memorial Reflecting Pool up to the Washington Monument, west to the river, and north to Constitution Ave. As you can see, we are at the base of the Washington Monument and our next move is north to the back fence of the White House. We have teams moving north on our east flank and they are encountering some resistance, but minor. We have them surrounded."

"Good, make it so, I am just here to confront that Nazi pig sitting in the White House," Pride stated. "This is your show, Colonel."

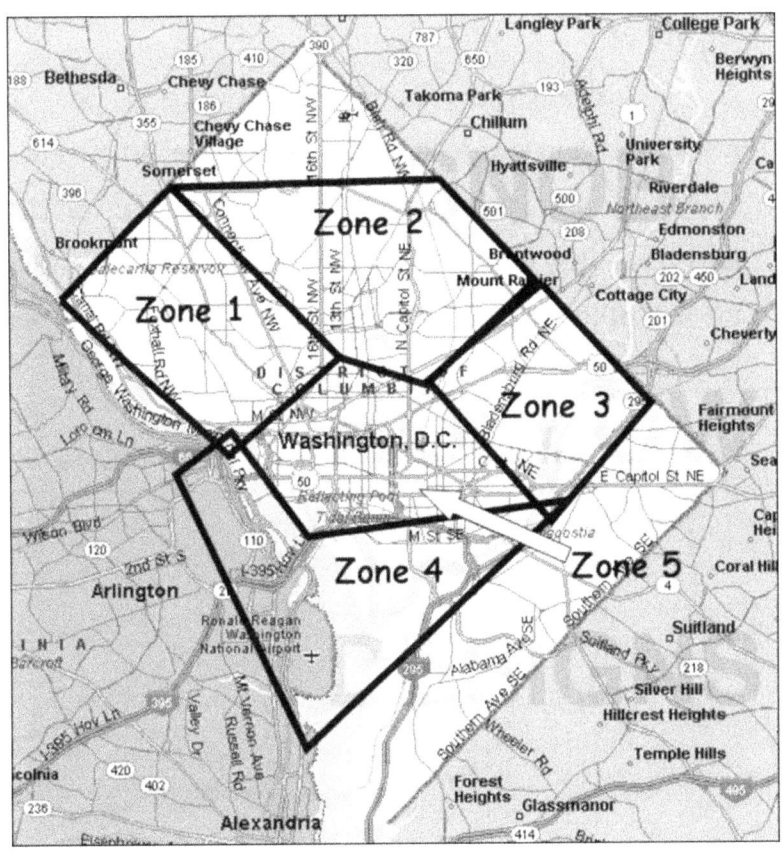

Battle Zone Map of Washington D.C.

Chapter 43 Pride's Quest

   Colonel Griffin, accompanied by General Pride, slowly moved the team toward the south fence of the White House. They knew the resistance around the White House would be heavy, and they were not disappointed. But his team, along with the help of the Special Forces team with General Pride, was hoping to be able to eliminate the resistance with ease.

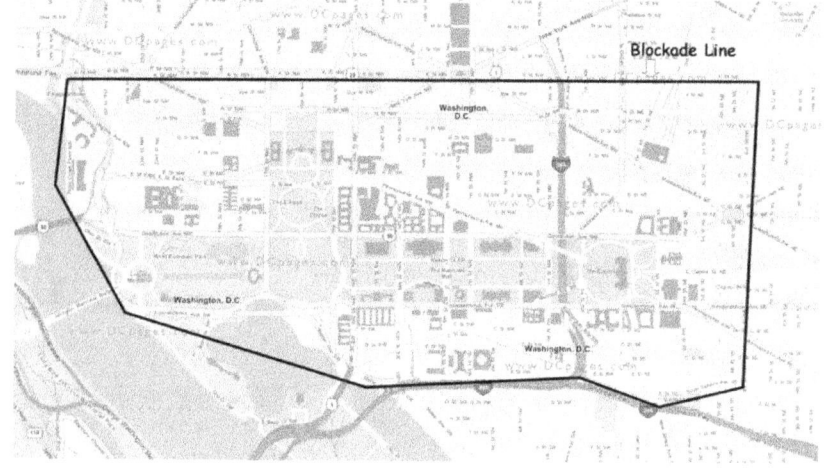

Area under Nazi control

   Reports were flowing into Griffin's headset that resistance around George Washington University was strong with the enemy held up in the dormitories and around the campus. Fighting was fierce, but the U.S. Forces were moving ahead. A report from the eastern front indicated that the capital building area was not as well defended, and the U.S. troops were quickly moving toward Zone Five and the White House. The biggest problem to solve was what to do with the prisoners they were taking. For every prisoner taken, they needed at least two guards; luckily, the Army Military Police were available to confine the prisoners on the front lawn of the Capital building in a make shift prison compound, which the Nazis had used to hold Americans when they were captured. Once the Americans were released, the Nazis were ushered into the compound.

Clearing each and every building in the Federal Triangle and all the museums located in the combat area would take time and a lot of men to complete, but the Army was completing the job as quickly as possible.

"Incoming!" yelled a sergeant as he ran past the World War II Memorial and dropped to the ground just as a mortar shell impacted the ground just over forty feet from him. All the soldiers near him also hit the ground; two were not lucky, as the shell landed very close to them, killing them instantly.

The sergeant saw from where the mortar was launched, and immediately aimed his CAR-16 in the direction and fired several three round bursts. At the same time, he called back to command to advise them of the mortar location with hopes of bringing fire down upon it before they were able to kill any more of his friends.

A minute and a half later, an Apache helicopter swooped in and fired two missiles at the location, immediately destroying the mortar launcher and the four Nazis working it. Heavy machine gun fire came from the corner of E Street and East Executive Avenue, which was the most southeastern corner of the White House property. They were shooting blind with hopes of hitting the Americans.

The fighting was sporadic, pockets of resistance were all around, but most of the Nazi invaders were not very motivated once they saw the American forces moving in precision toward them. They surrendered instead of fighting, but not all was so easy.

Griffin ordered a flanking movement that made it easier to eliminate the heavy machine gun on Executive Avenue. Moving in from the east with support from two M1A1 Abrams tanks, the enemy heavy machine gun immediately became vapor after one shot from the tank .

"All sectors report!" Griffin ordered as he looked at the White House through the southern fence.

Within minutes, he had the news he wanted; all zones were secure except for Zone Five. Each team was in the process of doing a building by building search for any Nazis that had not already been captured. The White House grounds were surrounded; all of the resistance was now just inside the fence. Troops from the 101st and 82nd Airborne were running sweeps through the buildings and rounding up Nazi fighters, the fighting was minimal. The overwhelming forces were backed up by a lot of M1A1 Abrams tanks.

This was not true of the elite forces surrounding the White House. Griffin had the White House surrounded, but was taking heavy fire from the Nazi forces protecting it.

"Bravo, Charlie teams, can you penetrate the E Street gates?" Griffin asked his team leads at E Street NE and NW gates.

"Blackfish, that's a negative. We are at the corner of E Street and 14th Street and are pinned down by heavy machine gun fire. And they have a tank," Bravo team lead responded, "Heavy fortification."

"Affirmative, Blackfish, but it's going to be a mess," Charlie team lead responded after he heard Bravo Team's response. "We are holding at the corner of E Street and 18th."

"We can rebuild the gate, take them out," Griffin ordered.

"Roger!" Bravo team lead responded, and then turned to his team sergeant and said, "Bring up the Abrams and take out that gate."

E Street becomes Pennsylvania Avenue once it leaves the White House grounds; Bravo Team had an M1 Abrams parked and waiting at the corner of Pennsylvania and 13th Street. Just two blocks away, the sergeant stopped beside his radio man and passed the order to him.

"Yes, sir," the team sergeant answered and then turned and moved quickly east to talk with the team's radio operator; the headsets they wore were only good for team member to team member communication. He needed to talk to the tank and they had their own frequencies. Seconds later, he reached the operator and had him switch to the frequency designated for armor and made the request to come forward and bring the noise. Meanwhile, due east of their position, Charlie team was doing the same thing. The Nazi position was about to understand why the United States military was someone you did not want to have on your bad side.

Lieutenant Nathan Kimble was the team lead for Bravo team; and when he heard the rumble of the Abrams coming up behind him, he just had to smile, knowing that those poor dumb Nazi sympathizers were about to taste the firepower of the Abrams M1A2 120 millimeter main gun.

At the gate on the east side of E Street, the Nazis heard and then saw the M1A2 turn the corner and level its main gun at them. Immediately, the Nazi machine gunners looked at each other briefly and smiled, knowing full well they were outgunned and were about to die. One of the Nazis reached over and picked up a walkie-talkie; after pressing the send button, he reported that their position was about to be overrun by the Americans.

Oval Office

Inside the Oval office, Gregory Dietrich took the news in stride. His messenger saluted and exited the Oval office as quickly as he had come in.

"Sergeant! Wait!" Dietrich yelled at the departing sergeant.

"Yes, sir," the sergeant said as he turned slowly to face his commander.

"Have they opened that elevator door yet?"

"No, sir, but we feel we are close, and there is no way they could have gotten out without seeing them."

"Get that door opened; now go," Dietrich yelled. As the sergeant exited the Oval Office, a young lieutenant entered and saluted.

"Yes Lieutenant."

"Sir, the south gates have been taken out and the Americans are approaching the building quickly. Our forces cannot stop them," the young lieutenant stated as he walked up to the desk.

"I expected that, just not this soon. We need to get that elevator opened," Dietrich stated and then looked at the picture on the wall of George Washington, the father of this country. "You know this country was started by a bunch of revolutionaries, they rebelled against a stronger adversary and won. These Americans are a tough bunch and I suppose we will die today, or if we are lucky, captured and sent to one of their nice prisons."

"Sir, we will be classified as terrorists and end up in a prison that is not very comfortable, do you want to go there?"

"No, but I am not ready to commit suicide like our leader, Adolf Hitler."

"I will get it opened, sir."

"Good, now go."

Main Gate

Griffin and General Pride were crouched down behind a tree in Lafayette Square looking intently at the main gate to the White House grounds. They had advanced to the north of the White House, securing the west side as they moved. The Nazis had placed a large moving truck across the entrance and had several heavy machine guns strategically placed to cover the field of fire able to cut down anyone who was foolish enough to attempt to storm the gate. Unknown to Griffin and Pride, there was also a T-34 Soviet tank parked behind the moving truck. About one hundred feet to the east of Griffin, his executive officer was seeing a similar setup at the eastern gate.

"Blackfish, this is Junior; we have a situation here, possibly similar to what you have there. What's the plan?" Griffin's Executive Officer asked over the secure network.

"General, what do you think? It's been pretty easy up till now," Griffin asked General Pride.

"Well, this is your party, remember; I am just a party crasher. But if you are asking for my opinion, and I have never been one to shy away from giving it," General Pride said, took a

243

breath and continued, "I believe we should bring up Charlie and have him blow away that truck and anyone near it."

"Really, sir? Charlie tends to make a very big mess of things. I believe I want to try something a little less messy."

"This I have to see."

"Watch and learn, sir," Griffin said and then clicked his microphone and spoke rapidly with his special team located on the roof of the Old Executive Building and on the east side on the roof of the Department of the Treasury. Unknown to Pride was that the two teams Griffin was talking to consisted of four snipers and half of each team was each armed with fifty caliber Barrett rifles with hi-intensity scopes and the other half were using 300 Winchester Magnums shooting 7.62 x 67mm rounds. Each shooter had a spotter that assisted in picking targets of opportunity. The snipers had loaded special fifty caliber rounds that were armor piercing and would explode once they penetrated the armor or wall.

As soon as Griffin finished ordering his snipers to fire, they could hear the report of the fifty caliber Barrett's blast. Nazis started running as fast as they could away from the gate, diving for cover behind concrete walls to no avail. With the infrared imaging on the scope, the snipers could see the heat signature of the Nazis behind the walls, and they just shot through the wall killing whoever was behind it.

"Impressive, Colonel, Impressive," General Pride said smiling.

Ten minutes passed, and the snipers had finished firing. They continued to scan the gates but saw no movement.

"Blackfish, cleared to move," Sergeant First Class Jeremy Davis, aka Trigger, reported over the secure net.

"Thanks, Trigger. Cover our advance," Griffin ordered and then to the men behind him he ordered, "Move out!"

The entire team started to move rapidly across Pennsylvania Ave toward the main gate and the eastern front gate. A few shots from the White House struck the wall and the street around them, but no hits reported. Reaching the gate, they immediately saw the destructive power of the Barrett rifle in the hands of a trained sniper with the exploding ammunition.

"Damn, those guys are good," Pride commented as they entered the White House grounds.

"We are not there yet, sir," Griffin said as they knelt behind the wall and looked at the White House with infrared binoculars. "I count two in the Oval Office, about twenty plus roaming around the first floor and it looks like at least twenty in the residence." After pausing for a moment, Griffin clicked his microphone, "Bravo, Charlie teams, location?"

"Blackfish, we are at the tennis court moving slowly toward objective," Bravo team lead reported.

"Roger, keep moving. We will meet you inside," Blackfish reported.

"Roger." Bravo and Charlie teams moved closer, encountering heavy resistance.

General Pride, Colonel Griffin and their team slowly approached the front door and waited. They heard heavy fire coming from the back of the White House; and as they scanned with their infrared goggles, they were able to see the location of the Nazis inside. Quietly, Griffin signaled his men to spread out and prepare to breach the front door.

Chapter 44 Out to Sea, Out of Time

As Josh and Davin were headed toward the bridge to rejoin Mary, they felt a vibration on the deck plates. "Sounds like Blair and Henry got the engine running," Josh commented and looked up to see a large plume of black smoke belch from the stack. "Maybe we will get out of this alive."

"I don't have a good feeling about this," Davin said smiling.

"What?"

"I've always wanted to say that, but let's not jump to conclusions before we actually get this tub moving and find out exactly where we are," Davin concluded.

"Okay, I agree," Josh said as he opened the door to the bridge and stepped in. "Mary, anything new up here?"

"Yeah, Blair called up on the intercom and said they were able to get the engine running, but not sure how long it would last. It's in pretty bad shape and looks like someone tried to sabotage it before leaving the ship. Oh, we got the intercom working too," Mary commented as they walked in.

"Well, for now it is running. Did you find any charts in this wreck?"

"Over here. I did some calculations, and I believe, now I am not a navigator or pilot, just well trained in survival, that if my calculations are correct, it would put us about here," she said pointing to a spot she had marked with an 'X', which was about six hundred miles off the coast of Africa.

"Well, if that is correct, we would have a better chance on going east to get to some land where I can check in and get us a flight to Berlin," Josh said.

"I think we need to check that Blackhawk out a little closer. If it is fueled, it has the range to make it to the coast, refuel and then fly it to Berlin or a US military base," Davin suggested.

"I like your idea, but let's stay dry on this tub and start to the coast, get a bit closer and then fly off her," Josh replied.

"Okay boys, let's make sure my location is correct and then drive this to the coast. Or... Oh shit!" Mary said and then pointed out the window at a ship on the horizon. "We have company."

"Holy crap!" Josh said as he picked up a pair of binoculars that were sitting on the console. "They are heading straight for us. And they don't look like a friendly; they may be coming back to get the rest of their cargo. We can't let them have it."

"Blair, Henry, get up here, fast," Davin said into the intercom.

"On our way," Blair replied back. Minutes later, Blair and Henry entered the bridge, "What's up?"

"They are," Josh said pointing toward the ship on the horizon.

"Can we move?" Davin asked.

"Yes, just push that lever there to engage the engines; and unless they screwed up the steering, we should be able to move, not fast, but we will move," Blair commented as Josh pushed the lever forward to about a halfway down position, which should have the ship move at about six knots. Slowly the ship started to move; Josh grabbed the wheel and turned it hard left to take up a heading of one hundred degrees, hoping to use the current to help them move a bit faster. Looking down at the control panel which was partly destroyed, he located the speed indicator and the needle was slowly moving off zero toward two and then three knots. When it finally stopped at five knots, he smiled at his friends.

"Okay, gather up every weapon we can locate and all the ammunition available; we may need it," Josh ordered. "Blair, you, Davin and I need to go check out that Blackhawk. Mary, hold course one zero zero; and if you can get a little more speed out of her, go for it."

"What do you want me to do?" Henry asked.

"You are the most important person; you keep an eye on that ship out there and also scan three hundred sixty degrees to make sure they do not have company. There is a crow's nest if you want the best view."

"You got it, sir," Henry replied as he grabbed the binoculars and went out the door and headed for the crow's nest ladder. When he arrived and looked up, he almost fainted; what he saw was not what he expected. Hanging over the railing was a body, obviously shot multiple times. *'Damn another body,'* he thought.

"Let's check out that bird, we may need her," Davin said as he picked up an M-16 and headed for the door.

After walking into the cargo bay that held the Blackhawk, they were surprised to find the helicopter in perfect shape. Blair climbed into the cockpit and inspected the controls, switched on the power and checked fuel levels, battery levels, and all checked out. Fuel indicators showed full tanks. "This bird is ready for war; she has every imaginable weapon system mounted on her including the new Hellfire missile. If only we had these in Nam, we would have really kicked some butt."

"Yeah, a fleet of these and it would have been over in a week. No way, remember Viet Nam was a politician's war not a soldier's war. They would never have given these to us; it wasn't good for business. They wanted the war to drag on so they could sell more oil and make more war materials," Davin commented as he slid out from under the helicopter. "The Hellfire is mounted on the belly and looks very functional and deadly."

"Right on that, old friend," Josh agreed.

Twenty minutes after entering the bay, they were satisfied that the bird was airworthy and ready to go. They only needed to open the cargo bay cover and lift her out. That might be a problem.

"Let's check the hoist and make sure we can get this bird out of the house," Josh said as he ran up the steps to the main deck. Upon reaching the top, he exited and walked rapidly to the first crane. "Davin look for the controls to open the bay cover."

"Already found them," he replied and then activated the switch and watched as the cover started to slide open. "Does the crane work?"

"Don't know yet. Blair, can you fly that thing?"

"No problem, Josh. Flew Blackhawks for four years," Blair commented.

"Josh, Davin, look!" Mary yelled and pointed. They glanced up and saw Mary and Henry both pointing to the stern of the ship. They saw that the other ship was closing fast. Josh and Davin headed for the bridge to get a better view of the ship behind them. Upon entering the bridge, they saw Henry standing near the opposite door holding an AK-47.

"Pour on the coals, Mary," Josh yelled back.

"I wouldn't do that, Mary," Henry said from across the room.

"What did you say Henry?" Josh questioned as he and Davin both turned around to look at Henry. What they saw they could not believe. "Why are you pointing that gun at us?"

"Mr. Randal, we need to let those people catch this boat. It is the only way we can survive," Henry stated while he held an AK-47 at them.

"What do you mean, the only way we can survive?" Davin asked as he started to step sideways to put more distance between he and Josh.

"Stay where you are Mr. Pierce, I don't want to shoot any of you, but I will if I have to. Now call Captain Blair and get him up here."

"No, tell me what is going on Henry and put that gun down," Josh said as he slowly slid further away from Davin.

"I said don't move!" Henry said and pointed the AK-47 at Josh and pulled the trigger sending a short bust of three bullets at Josh. Josh was hit and flung backward into the bulkhead.

"What the HELL are you doing?" Davin yelled and quickly rushed over to his fallen friend. Lying on his side, Josh turned his head and looked up at Davin and winked. He closed his eyes and rolled back over. Davin just stared at his friend with disbelief. He stood and turned toward Henry with murder in his eyes. "He's dead," he said after a few seconds.

"Maybe now you will listen when I say don't move," he calmly stated as he leveled his weapon at Davin and Mary. "Now call down to Blair and get him up here, NOW!"

"Why, Henry?" Mary asked, "He was your friend."

"I have to, it's the only way," Henry yelled, tears starting to run down his face.

"Blair, come on up to the bridge," Davin called down to Blair who was preparing the helicopter, to ensure it would fly.

Chapter 45 Zone 5 Battle for the White House

Griffin signaled his lieutenant to open the door and to step back to let his men storm in. Seconds later, the door was flung open and twenty Special Forces soldiers charged in, shooting any Nazis they saw. After immediately dropping ten of the Nazis, they started a room to room search for any Nazis that might be attempting to hide.

Pride and Griffin walked over to the door to the Oval Office and stopped. "What do you think we will find sir?" Griffin asked as he reached for the door knob. He paused for a second before he turned the knob, "Ready."

"How did you get in here?" Dietrich asked as he saw Major General Pride walk through the door of the Oval Office. Standing tall in his Nazi uniform behind the President's desk, he was stunned to see the General and six armed soldiers walk in.

"That was easy; my question is what the hell do you think you are doing behind my President's desk in that outdated Nazi uniform?" Pride asked as he walked toward the President's desk. "Who do you think we are? No, I will answer that; we are Americans and we beat Hitler and your grandfather years ago. Didn't that tell you that we are the big dog on the porch and not to mess with us?" Pride fired back at Dietrich. "And don't even think about reaching for that antique Lugar on your waist. I really don't want to get blood on the President's carpet," he said as the soldiers raised their weapons and pointed them at Dietrich. "Sergeant please remove his weapon."

"General, we came to prove to your country that you are vulnerable to attack. We took over your government center within hours. You could not stop us; we succeeded, and you failed," Dietrich commented.

"Well, sir, it is now your failure; you are under arrest for crimes against the United States of America and will be treated as a war criminal and terrorist." He paused for a second and then looked at the sergeant standing behind Dietrich with the Lugar in his hand. "Cuff him, Sergeant, and get that scum out of this office. Before they take you to a holding pen, would you be so kind to order your men to stand down so we don't have to kill all of them."

"I need to use that radio, General. But with my hands cuffed I cannot do that," Dietrich commented as he looked down at the hand held radio lying on his desk.

"Sergeant, operate it for him," Griffin ordered.

"Yes, sir," the sergeant replied and picked up the radio, studied it for a second and then held it up to Dietrich mouth. "Go ahead and speak, I will push the button."

"Attention, attention, this is General Dietrich; I order you to stand down and surrender to the American soldiers. Do not continue fighting. I say again, stand down and surrender to the American forces. We have succeeded in our quest and they now have control of the city," Dietrich ordered and then listened as each of the remaining forces responded with 'Affirmative.' He got two 'negatives'.

"You are ordered to stand down. No questions, just do it. They will kill you if you don't stand down. No more fighting, stand down, NOW!"

"No sir, we will kill all Americans, you are no longer our commander," came the reply over the radio.

"You heard him, General. I guess your men will have to kill them," Dietrich said to General Pride.

"Captain, call our troops and tell them the Nazis are surrendering; if any resist, then kill them. Have them captured, if possible; otherwise, eliminate them," Colonel Griffin ordered and then walked over to Dietrich and stared at him for a moment before signaling his sergeant to take him away.

"Yes, sir, right away," the Captain said and started to walk out of the Oval Office to make the call on the command radio located in the foyer.

"Wait, I see that your men were working on the elevator in this hallway, what were they expecting to find if they were able to get it opened?" Pride asked stopping the Captain and Dietrich.

"It has to be the entrance to your country's bunker; the place where your President ran to save his own ass and left his country to fend for itself," Dietrich commented, paused for a second and then stated, "He is a coward."

"Is that so, Mr. Dietrich?" President Mitchell said as he entered his Oval Office.

"Mr. President, you shouldn't have come back so soon; we have not completely secured the building," Griffin said as President Mitchell walked over behind his desk.

"And you were smoking my cigars!" Mitchell said as he looked at the mess on his desk and around the office. "You have made a mess of my city, my home and my office, Mr. Dietrich, and you will pay dearly for your transgressions."

"Your country is vulnerable to attack; and we succeeded in taking over your city within hours without losing fifty men.

And you call your country powerful, what a lie!" Dietrich exclaimed as he stared at Mitchell.

"Yes, you proved to us that we are vulnerable, and we will make sure it will never happen again. We did take it back from you before you did too much damage. Our forces are stronger, better trained and better equipped. Your kind is a dying breed; and when your trial is over, it will be my honor to throw the switch to fry your ass. Get him out of my office, Captain," Mitchell said without blinking an eye.

Almost all of Dietrich's men started to lay down their weapons after hearing the announcement; there were a few hold outs. As the Americans moved in to collect the weapons and round up the prisoners, there were several fire fights that resulted in the death of a couple of Nazis and fourteen wounded Americans. They were not able to capture the hold outs, so they sent them to visit hell.

Minutes later, a Special Forces Master Sergeant entered the Oval Office to report that forty-six Nazi infiltrators had been captured and eight were killed while resisting capture in the White House. He had his men escort them to the lawn behind the White House and guarded until they were able to move them to a more secure holding area.

"Thank you Master Sergeant," Griffin said and then turned to General Pride and said to the President, "Sir, your home is secure."

"Get the bomb squad in here to ensure they did not leave any surprises for us," Pride requested.

"Already in the works, sir," Griffin replied, smiling.

Pride just smiled. "Mr. President, we will leave this team here to protect you until the bomb squad has cleared the building. If they say move, please do so."

Chapter 46 Recovery

"Mr. Pierce, please move his body off the bridge," Henry ordered.

"Mary, grab his feet please," Davin asked politely. Mary moved over and bent down to pick up Josh's feet as Davin reached under his arms, carrying Josh to the radio room located at the back of the bridge. Mary being a very efficient flight steward quickly noticed that Josh had a pulse in his ankle and she also felt that he still had his backup pistol strapped to his left inside ankle. Looking up at Davin, she almost smiled at the discovery, but kept her demeanor.

Henry kept his weapon trained on Davin and Mary, but also kept his eye on the bridge doors for the arrival of Blair.

"Ms Mary, to answer your question as to why, well, that is simple, self preservation," Henry replied but not smiling. "This nutcase has my family, and he promised that my family would not be harmed in anyway. He has my wife and kids. Says he is the head of a Nazi organization that has ties all over the world. You see, I have a good reason to make you disappear. Before we left the States, I got a call and was told that a team of his men would pick us up; and once you were dead, they would release my family and me too. So, you see, you all have to die; but I will not kill you, they will, after, well, after whatever they do to you. I am sorry about Mr. Randal, but I didn't trust him. We just need to sit tight until our ride gets here."

A minute later, Blair walked onto the bridge and saw Davin and Mary sitting at the computer console with Henry pointing his weapon at them and then quickly moved it toward Blair.

"What is going on here, where is Josh" Blair asked as he entered the bridge.

"This is a mutiny, Mr. Blair. And you are now my prisoner. Behave yourself, and you will not end up like Mr. Randal," Henry stated between tears. "Please take a seat; we have some time before the boat arrives." He reached over and pulled the engine throttle back to stop.

"Henry, if they have your family, we can help you get them back safely. You don't have to do this. Josh did not have to die, and neither do we. As far as that goes, do you really think they will just release you and your family after we are dead. They will eliminate any and all witnesses. Think about it Henry, they can't have any witnesses, which means you are already dead; your body just doesn't know it yet."

"No! No, they promised they were going to let us go as soon as you were dead."

"They are Nazis; they killed millions during World War II, just because they were Jewish. Do you really think they will just turn you lose so you can tell the world what they did. No way man, they will kill you as soon as you get on that boat. Your family is probably already dead, hopefully not. But we will never know, since we will be dead, too."

"Nice try Mr. Pierce; they promised my family would remain safe as long as I did what I did."

"So exactly what have you done so far?" Davin asked. "Let's see, you sabotaged our plane which caused us to crash in the middle of the ocean, way off course from what I have seen. That would make it easy for your Nazi friends to find us and not be disturbed. They did not plan on one of their freighters being here also, just luck of the draw, I guess. Oh, and there is the thing about shooting Josh, my best friend and boss. Killing him bought you the death penalty if we are rescued before your friends arrive."

"That sounds about right, Mr. Pierce. Except I did not sabotage our plane, one of the ground crew did that; I had nothing to do with it. I didn't even know what they did until it happened. They told me they would do something and I should be on the lookout. I guess they didn't expect us to live through the crash. I guess I am dead either way, if I surrender to you I will go to jail and possibly die in the electric chair; if I follow through with turning you over ,you say they will kill me and my family. Either way I am a dead man."

"Yes, you are correct. But think of it this way; if you surrender yourself to us, we will do our best to keep you from the death penalty. You are under stress, and they have threatened you and your family."

Henry had his back to the starboard bridge door and did not hear the footsteps coming up behind him.

"Henry, please lay down your weapon and slowly turn around," Josh Randal said quietly as he walked up behind Henry.

"It can't be; you are dead.," Henry said as he turned and saw Josh standing in front of him with a Glock Model 30 forty-five caliber pistol pointing at him.

"The report of my death has been greatly exaggerated. Yes, I am hurt, but not dead yet, anyway," Josh commented. Davin quickly stood and picked up the weapon that Henry had laid on the deck.

"Glad to see you up and about, old friend," Davin said to his friend and then took Henry by the shoulder and sat him down in the chair he had just vacated. "Henry we can forget what you have done if you agree to help us get out of here alive. And we will do our best to save your family as soon as we get back."

"You will do that?" Henry asked unsure of his future.

"Yes, we can do that, can't we, Josh?" Davin stated.

"Sure, but I do think I need a little medical care, Mary, can you help me?" Josh said as he slowly collapsed to the deck. Mary got up and ran over to Josh, kneeling down and pulled open his shirt.

"Captain, get me a med kit, quickly. He is bleeding, and will not be with us long if I don't stop it," Mary ordered as she examined the bullet wounds. Two had passed right through Josh's right shoulder, but the third was a bit more severe. Stopping the bleeding was her first concern; the two shoulder wounds had not hit any vital organs or bones as far as she could tell. The third hit was inches away from his heart just below his right nipple. The bullet had struck a rib and broke it, ricocheted up, and lodged itself in his shoulder blade preventing him from moving his right arm.

Twenty minutes later, Mary stopped and looked up at Davin, Blair and Henry and with her eyes fixed on Henry with a lot of hate in them she quietly said, "Henry Theodore Radcliff, you should be ashamed of yourself. You could have killed him."

"I am sorry, Mary, I don't know what got into me. Lucky for Josh I am a bad shot," Henry apologized almost smiling that Josh would live.

"I hate to put a damper on your apology Henry, but I do believe we have company, are you on our side or theirs? We need all the fire power we can get, and if I have to tie you up that only leaves three of us to defend this tub. Josh will be out of it for a while and we could use you," Blair asked as he was scanning the horizon and spotted a large ocean going yacht headed in their direction. "Looks like about a one hundred twenty foot cruiser, could carry up to one hundred Nazis, or we could get lucky and there is only a small team on board."

"Henry?" Davin asked as he looked at Henry.

"I am with you, promise," Henry agreed.

"I will not hesitate to shoot you if you should change your mind, and I shoot to kill," Davin stated. "Now pick up that AK-47 and grab a couple more mags. You will stay here with me. Mary and Captain Blair, go down and get that helo ready to take off. I want to be in the air before they get here; we should have about forty minutes from the looks of it. Now go."

Chapter 47 If You Only Knew

Washington D.C. was now back under the control of the American people. Her president had moved back into the White House after having safely lived and governed from the bunker known as Mount Weather.

"Good morning Mr. President," National Security Advisor Tony Sanford said as he entered the Oval Office.

"How long before the repairs are completed on our home, Tony?" President Mitchell asked from behind his desk, a desk he had lost for a few days to a band of Nazi sympathizers. He was reading reports from around the country, describing the destruction and repair of the cities that had been damaged. The one he was most concerned with was the report from Cyber Command. The report confirmed his belief that the country was still very vulnerable to attack from anyone that had a computer. His concerns were justified from the report, the country had suffered a lot and he was tired. His administration had had the worst time over the past three years.

"When are you going to address the nation; they want to hear that the country is safe and they can go about their lives without worry of someone dropping a bomb on them," Tony commented without a smile.

"If they only knew how bad we are. But they don't want to hear that. I have my speech writers working on a speech. I will not lie to them, but I can't tell the entire truth; there would be panic and more riots," Mitchell stated.

"Yes, I know, so sugar-coat it. They don't need to know everything. But they need to know we are working on putting the country back together," Tony agreed as he picked up his coffee and took a sip.

"Hell, we are politicians; they know when we are lying, and every time our mouth is open we are lying. You know that, well, maybe you don't; you have only been a politician for a couple of years and have not learned all the bad things they say about us."

"Yeah, I know all the things they say about politicians; some of it isn't pretty, but, what the hell, we do what we have to do. And your term in this office has seen a lot of crap and the people will see that you have done a great job. It was impossible to predict what was going to happen; you did what you did and should be proud of it. Now, let's talk about what we need to do next."

"Next, after the State of the Union speech tonight, we need to re-allocate some funds to help rebuild what we can. Boston will not be the same for a hundred years and Denver also has a hot zone. Not much we can do with them; the rest of the country has repairs going. Cyber Command is in the process of rebuilding and getting reestablished. They are taking a temporary home at Fort Bragg; they feel they will be safer there, at least until McDill is rebuilt," Mitchell stated and dropped the report he was reading on his desk. "Tony, my term will be up next year, and I am not going to run again. I want to spend time with my daughter. Remember her, cute little thing, looks a lot like her mom. With the loss of her mom and my being kidnapped, well, we need to spend some time together just to relax."

"I understand, but I don't think you should make up your mind just yet," Tony stated and then changed the subject. "Look…"

A knock on the door stopped the conversation. Tony stood and walked over to the door and opened it. "What brings you down here, General Pride?" he asked when he saw General Pride standing on the other side. "Come in."

"President Mitchell asked me to stop by. I hope you don't mind, but Colonel Griffin is with me."

"Come on in General Pride and Colonel Mitchell. Please help yourself to some coffee and have a seat; we need to talk a bit, nothing bad, just need some clarification," Mitchell stated.

"Sir I will be right back, I need to run to my office and get a file," Sanford said and then stepped out of the office.

"Hurry back, Tony," Mitchell said as Sanford left the office.

"How can I be of service to you sir?" Pride asked as he poured himself some coffee.

"First, I want to thank you and Colonel Griffin for not destroying the White House and for saving our city," Mitchell commented as he started to sit on the sofa across from Griffin and Pride.

"Sir, it was a pleasure to assist, but the thanks goes to my men; they made it happen. We just came along for the ride," Griffin commented.

"A lot has happened over the past couple of days, part of which you were involved in and we do not need to discuss that anymore. What I tell you in this office cannot be discussed with anyone outside this office. Understand?" Mitchell began just as he heard a soft knock on the door. "Come in Tony."

271

Tony Sanford stepped into the Oval Office and greeted the President and his guests.

"I am about to disclose the project to them; you have the file now? Jump in, if I miss anything," Mitchell said and then took a long drink from his coffee cup. "We have been nuked, attacked by Nazis, bombed by the North Koreans and Chinese terrorists, and yet we still survive. This proves once again that we are the greatest nation on the planet. We have lost citizens and we will possibly lose more to the radiation that is drifting around the country. The doctors are working overtime to prevent more deaths. Our biggest problem is we are Americans and Americans don't give up, do we? Boston and Denver were the worst hit, millions of our citizens have died doing what they believed was just another day in their life. Saying all that, I need to be very specific about the rest of this conversation. I am about to order the two of you to do something that no other president has had the nerve to do. I am going to order you to start a war, but not just any war, a war that we will win. Not another Viet Nam or Desert Storm or even Afghanistan. Let me explain, I want you to put together an operational plan to end the war in Afghanistan, remove Iran's nuclear arsenal and clean up Iraq. When I say end it, I mean just that. I want our troops to come home, but I don't want any terrorist group to think they can kill Americans or for that matter any other person that does not believe in what they believe. And before you say anything, yes, I still believe in free speech, freedom of religion and the pursuit of happiness; but I also believe that these terrorists only believe they should rule the world and have no respect for life, even their own."

"We are already in those countries and are holding our own, not winning or losing. You want us to make it so we win and they lose. That, sir, is impossible. The war there is not like any conventional war, even more so than Viet Nam. They do not play by any rules, using kids, women and not caring about collateral damage; killing Americans and non-believers is all they care about. They soak up on drugs before blowing themselves up, killing as many Americans as they can. How the hell are we supposed to stop that?" Pride asked.

"Yes General, all those things are happening now and will continue as long as they can find volunteers to join their ranks. Now it may seem impossible and probably is. Limit the collateral damage as much as possible to eliminate them. But we need to redirect resources into repairing our country and quit spending it fighting a war that can't be won. Almost like Viet Nam, but at least we knew who the enemy was," Mitchell

273

agreed. "Your job is to come up with a way we can withdraw in a win situation from all three countries."

"That is almost like genocide, sir. You are talking like Hitler and I can't be a part of that," Griffin commented shaking his head.

"Not quite, but maybe close. I don't want you to carpet bomb the country and kill everyone; I don't know how we are going to do it. Sorting out the innocents from the insurgents is going to be difficult, but I know we can do it," Mitchell stated looking sternly at both commanders.

"The Rules of Engagement need to be reworked; right now they hinder our movement a lot," Pride commented and looked at Griffin with a questionable eye.

"We can put our minds together and see what we can come up with. Do we have access to whatever we need to make this plan viable?" Griffin asked. "And, I agree, the rules need to be reworked, sir."

"Part of your job is to rework the Rules of Engagement. I want a plan on my desk in a week. Can you do it?" Mitchell asked.

"We will do our best, sir."

"That's all I ask, General."

Chapter 48 New Mission for an Old Blackhawk

"Davin, we have a problem," Blair said over the radio to Davin on the bridge.

"What is it, Blair?"

"This bird was built in 1980 and she looks airworthy; but these engines are the original, and according to the log book, she hasn't been serviced in at least four years. I will do what I can to ensure we get off the deck, but I cannot promise how long she will fly," Blair stated.

"Do what you can Blair. It is either fly that old bird off the deck or die for sure from those pirates closing on us," Davin said as he watched Blair raise the Blackhawk on its pad out of the cargo hold and up to the deck. The deck crane was working perfectly, and he was able to set the pad down on the deck gently. "How much longer?"

"Ten minutes," Blair replied.

"You have about five, make it a quick ten; we are about to have company. Henry and I are heading down," Davin said and then turned to Henry, "Are you ready?"

"Yes, sir. Sorry about Mr. Randal."

"He will live, help me carry him down to the helo," Davin said as he slung his weapon over his shoulder and reached down to pick up Josh. Henry took Josh's other arm and they headed for the door just as several bullets slammed into the side of the bridge. "Damn, we are in range; let's get moving."

They headed down the ladder to the lower deck, staying on the port side of the bridge tower to keep from being shot. Minutes later, they approached the Blackhawk and slid Josh into the back seat and strapped him in. Blair was in the cockpit going through the preflight checklist; moments later, the main rotor started to spin, slowly at first, then faster and faster. Blair signaled to Mary to unhook the tie down from the helo and to climb on board. Once she was in and Henry was in the co-pilot seat, Blair confirmed that everyone was strapped in and then twisted the cyclic and lifted the Blackhawk off the deck.

"I see you loaded the M-240 machine gun; good move, Blair," Davin commented as he stood and hooked the safety strap to himself, and moved the M-240 around to check full movement. The M-240 replaced the M-60 machine gun developed by Fabrique Nationale (FN) U.S. Ordnance, Inc. used as a general-purpose machine gun. It fired the 7.62mm round at a rate of seven hundred fifty to nine hundred fifty rounds per minute, with a muzzle velocity of two thousand eight hundred feet per second. It was lighter than its predecessor which was one of the reasons the U.S. Military adopted it. It had been in service since 1977 and was used by the US Armed Forces during the Gulf War, Iraq War and War in Afghanistan. "What else is working on this bird?"

"She has missiles, but not sure if they will launch. However, if need be, we will try," Blair commented just as several bullets slammed into the side of the Blackhawk. "Taking fire, I suggest we return the favor, don't you think, Davin?" "I do; swing us around and I will check the aim on this old gun," Davin commented as he clicked off the safety and pulled the charging handle to put a round in the chamber. As they came around and he had a clear target, he pulled the trigger and watched as the bullets splashed in the water around the boat. He continued the same rate of fire with more splashes and several hit the speeding boat causing the driver to turn sharply to avoid being hit again.

"Enough fun, get us out of here Blair," Davin ordered.

"Roger that, low and fast," Blair replied and then turned the Blackhawk toward the east and dropped to fifty feet off the water and ran up to just under one hundred fifty miles per hour.

He did not want to push the old bird too hard, her max speed was rated at one hundred eighty-four, but that was in like new condition; this bird was over thirty years old and not serviced well.

The pirate boat was left smoking, but still afloat; they managed to reach the freighter and board it, only to be stranded on board watching their one hundred twenty foot power boat slowly sink under the waves.

"Nice shooting, Davin."

"How long before we reach land?" Davin asked and before he got an answer he turned to Mary, "Take a look at Josh; he is not looking good."

"Not much I can do, but I will check his bandages," Mary replied.

"If we are able to stay in the air, we should hit land in about an hour and a half, if my calculations are correct. Anyway, either way, we should be in the air for less than two hours," Blair replied.

"Less than two hours?" Davin questioned.

"That's about all the fuel we have, sorry. But it is either land or we get wet again," Blair stated.

"I would prefer not crashing in the ocean again; one swim with the sharks is enough for me this week."

"Think positive Davin, we will make land," Blair said confidently.

"I am positive I don't want to swim with the sharks again; get us to land," Davin requested.

"Ship on the horizon, should we check it out and see if they are friendly," Blair yelled back.

After picking up a pair of binoculars Davin had relieved from the freighter, he looked at the ship and commented, "Looks like a war ship. Too far away to determine who they are, head toward them and let's see if these old radios work."

Blair switched the primary radio to the standard guard frequency which every U.S. aircraft used and most Navy monitored. "Unidentified warship on course two five zero, this is Blackhawk Helo seven six four, on guard, please respond," Blair announced several times over the radio. Receiving no response, he turned to Davin and said, "No response."

"Keep trying," Davin answered and then to Henry he said, "Henry, arm the missiles please."

"Yes sir," Henry replied and started flipping switches to arm the two missile launchers.

"Unidentified Blackhawk seven six four, this is *U.S.S. Anzio*; you are kind of far from shore, how can we help?" a voice replied over the guard frequency.

"Anzio, that is a long story; we are low on fuel and engines running rough. Would it be possible to land on your helo pad and we can explain everything."

"Identify your crew and give us a good reason to believe you are not hostile," the voice answered.

"One moment, sir," Blair said and then leaned over and indicated for Davin to take over the conversation.

"This is Davin Pierce, Assistant Director of Covert Operations for the CIA. You can check with operations to…"

"Hold on sir, we have been looking for you. Stand by; the commander wants to talk to you," the radio operator said and then handed the microphone to her commander.

"Mr. Pierce, is your team still together?"

"Mostly, Randal has been shot and needs medical attention."

"Have your pilot come up behind us and land on pad; disarm all weapons before landing and I will meet you on the pad."

"Thank you sir, see you in a few minutes."

Chapter 49 Cannes, France Revisited

"What the hell just happened?" Polson asked nobody in particular.

"I think Ms Kim just killed the General," Amber Miller said as she pulled her weapon and started toward the chalet. The team immediately ran for the house, weapons drawn; and once through the gate, they split up with two heading to the left, two agents to the right, and Polson with Miller headed for the front door. Reaching it in seconds, they found it locked. The door was massive and would not open with a kick to the lock. They stepped to the right and found a window, broke it, reached in and unlocked it. Sliding it open, they climbed carefully through it and immediately saw the General laying in a pool of blood in the foyer.

As they leaned over the body, the other four agents entered the foyer.

"No luck sir, the back door was open, and the house is empty," one of the agents commented as he looked at the body.

"Check the boat house," Polson ordered.

"Be right back, sir," one of the agents said and then grabbed another agent and headed out the back toward the boat house.

"Two shots to the chest and one to the head, confirming the kill; she was serious about taking him out. Ms Peterson said we should watch for something like this. You do know why we were watching this guy?" Polson stated.

"Yes, he was the guy who fired eight nuclear missiles at America. Why didn't we just arrest him when we got here?" Amber commented.

"Agent Polson, no boat down there, she and her guys must have taken it. There was the sound of a boat speeding away, most likely her," the agent reported.

"Thanks, get on the phone and call the local police; have them put out a BOLO for Ms Kim and her friends. Tell them we are here and will wait until they arrive," Polson ordered and then turned his attention back to Amber, "We were hoping the people who paid him were going to show up, but I guess that isn't going to happen or maybe they did and this was the payment," Polson commented, then stood and pulled out his cell phone, and pressed speed dial 1.

"Ms Peterson, this is John Polson, is she in?" Polson asked after three rings and it was picked up by Helen, Ashley's assistant.

"Just a moment, please," Helen said.

"Hello John, what have you got?" Ashley asked.

"Shin is dead."

"Dead, thought she might do that; did you catch her?"

"No, she took off in a boat that was in the boat house."

"Where did she get a boat?"

"There must have been one in the Chalet's boat house. She is gone; we have contacted the local police to be on the lookout for her at the airports, train and bus stations," Polson stated.

"John, there was no way you could have prevented Shin's killing. Pack up your team and come home. Kim is gone, and she will not be using any commercial means to exit the country; she probably has a private jet waiting with engines running. They are most likely already in the air."

"You are right, Ashley. We will catch the next flight out."

"No, go to the nearest Air Force Base; there will be a flight waiting for you. They will bring you and your team directly to Andrews Air Force Base. See you in a few hours;

report directly to me when you get back and bring Amber with you." And then she hung up the phone.

"Okay, bye," Polson said to a dead line and then hung up. Not many miles away at Aeroport Cannes, Mandelieu sat in a Gulfstream VI corporate jet just spooling up its engines. Kim and her body guards ran the small fast speed boat south around the marina and the west to a small marina just south of the Airport. After docking the speed boat, they walked to a black Suburban, climbed in and were taken to the general aviation side of the airport where they climbed on board their jet.

Once on board, the jet requested immediate departure and started to taxi to the end of runway three five, where it waited until they got their clearance. And the jet then rolled onto the runway and started its takeoff roll, gaining speed and rotated, climbing to thirty five thousand feet and turned southeast for their flight to Pyongyang, North Korea. Kim and her guards sat back to enjoy a cocktail and a meal as they flew home, the flight would take almost nineteen hours only stopping to refuel.

Kim smiled; she had accomplished her mission without too much trouble. Her only loss was the contact she had in the CIA; she had been a good contact, providing a lot of good information. But it was worth the trade; Shin had betrayed her country and he needed to die. But there was another mole, and he would be much better. He was in a position within the file room, having access to every classified document they produced. It was his job to maintain the files. He hadn't turned yet, but he would, with the right incentives. And she was good at getting incentives.

Chapter 50 *USS Anzio*

"Good afternoon lady and gentlemen, the commander is waiting for you in the war room; please follow me. The corpsmen will take Mr. Randal to the doctor," the Lieutenant Commander said as he greeted the crew of the Blackhawk. "Our ground crew will secure your bird." And then as he turned to the lead ground crew Chief, he said, "Get the techs to go over that bird; make sure she is ready to fly again; refuel and do whatever is necessary to fight if need be."

"Reload the guns?" the chief questioned.

"Yes."

"Yes, sir," the chief responded.

"Follow me," the Lieutenant Commander said to the Blackhawk crew.

"Right behind you, Commander," Davin said as they walked toward the hatch leading to the war room.

"Come in and take a seat. There are sandwiches and drinks on the table, help yourself," the Captain said as they were lead into the war room. He was pacing across the front of the room where there was a projected picture of Gregory Dietrich in a Nazi uniform on the wall.

"Who is that?" Davin asked as he picked up a sandwich and soda.

"I will explain everything that has happened while you were enjoying a little ocean cruise," the Captain explained. "First, I am Captain Lewis Adams, and welcome to the *USS Anzio*. We have been looking for you since your plane disappeared."

"We thank you for not giving up on us," Blair commented.

"Now you need to know what has been going on over the past week. You are not going to believe the story I am about to tell you." Captain Adams started; twenty minutes later, he finished his story of the invasion of a large Nazi army attacking and taking over Washington D.C. and the eventual retaking of the city by members of the 101st and 82nd Airborne troops and members of the US Marines under the command of Major General Pride. He confirmed that Hans Bormann was dead; his body was found in a burned out warehouse south of Berlin. The picture on the screen was identified as Gregory Dietrich, commander of the Nazi forces. He is presently cooling his heals in a Federal Prison along with most of his attacking force. They will be formally charged with war crimes against the United

States within a few weeks; until then, they are all in military prisons around the country.

"Wow, that is one hell of a story," Davin commented and then looked over at Henry and Mary.

"I am glad we missed that," Mary said and then took a sip of coke.

"Look what happens when we go out of town for a few days," Davin joked.

"Yeah, you and Randal leave town and all hell breaks loose," Blair agreed.

"Guess we need to stay in town to keep the peace," Davin said and then changed the subject. "Captain, that freighter is carrying military weapons including that Blackhawk and crates of Hellfire Missile systems. We need to get back over there before they get that freighter to their base and unload those weapons."

"We will be heading in that direction as soon as we know which direction. Our own helo is out scouting for that freighter, and so far, we are not having much luck. Captain Blair, what was your heading to reach us?"

"Zero two five," Blair answered.

"Okay, our helo started out on the reciprocal of that heading and found nothing, yet. We are still looking," Captain Adams replied shaking his head. "This is a big ocean and there are no islands where they can hide. If they are out there, we will find them. In the meantime, why not enjoy our hospitality, and get some rest. When we find them, we will let you know. They can't go far; from what you told me, it was not running very well. But with all that military cargo, they must have a plan and a place to go."

"I agree, Captain. If you want, after your men finish with that old Blackhawk, I can take her up and help with the search; just supply me with a crew. Henry is a great pilot, but I would like a helo pilot. He is a jet pilot and not helo. Is that a problem, Henry?"

"No, Captain, I would rather sit it out on this boat, a qualified helo pilot would be best if you get into a firefight anyway," Henry agreed.

"Okay, Captain Blair, why don't you go down and get some rest; we will have your bird ready in an hour and I have a very good Blackhawk pilot and crew for you. They have been waiting for a chance to go blow up something or at least chase some bad guys," Captain Adams said and then turned to Lt.

Commander and said, "Take these good people to our guest quarters, and see that they are comfortable. If they need something more substantial to eat, take them to the mess and get chief to fix them whatever they want."

"Aye, aye, sir," to his captain and to Davin's team, "Follow me," the Lt Commander said and got up and headed for the door.

Chapter 51 Is This the End?

Walter Reed Hospital

Josh Randal lay sleeping in Walter Reed Military Hospital room 265 with multiple wires and tubes stuck in him. His vital signs were stable, and the bullets had been removed by the doctor on board the *USS Anzio*. His recovery would take a while, but he needed a break anyway; and why not rest and get paid at the same time. The CIA had a pretty good medical plan, and he was collecting on all the money he had put in over the years. But he felt cheated; he missed out on the search for the freighter. Even though they did not find it, he would have enjoyed the search. He missed out on finding Hans Bormann, who he recently found out was dead, killed most likely by his own boss, Gregory Dietrich. Now he lay here sucking up some pain killers and wishing he was back in his office.

"Connie, we need to go by the hospital and check on Josh," Davin said as he was looking at his young family.

Home of Davin and Connie Pierce

"Stephanie called this morning; she said he was doing well. I will get Nancy over to watch the kids after dinner," Connie replied as she placed her daughter into her crib.

"By the way, what is for dinner?"

"Steak and potato, a little red wine and salad," she said with a smile.

"I didn't see any steak in the kitchen."

"I know; we are going to meet Stephanie at your favorite steak house and then go over to the hospital together," Connie stated.

"Fine by me, when does Nancy get here?"

"She is downstairs waiting for us to leave. Grab your jacket and let's go," she said and then headed for the door and down the stairs. "Nancy, we are leaving now; the kids are asleep, and we should be back in a couple of hours. If you need anything, please call me," Connie said as she headed for the front door.

As they drove to the restaurant, Connie had some questions she could not ask with Nancy in the house. They were not classified, but sensitive in nature.

"Davin, how is the witch hunt going?" she asked referring to the hunt of the mole within the agency.

"I don't know. When I talked to Ashley this morning, she was working on confirming that the information we received was accurate," Davin said as he drove toward the steak house.

"How much longer do you think it will take?"

"Don't know," he said and turned into the steak house. He saw Stephanie's car and parked next to it. "After we check on Josh, let's stop by the agency; I need to check on a few things. At least, whoever it is, they are not selling secrets anymore because Kim cut off the money flow."

"Okay, as long as we are not too late; Nancy has school tomorrow."

The steaks were good; and after paying the bill, they headed for Walter Reed. The ride would take about thirty minutes with light traffic. After seeing Josh and talking to his doctor, they were satisfied that he would fully recover. He was expected to be released in about a week. Connie and Davin then left and headed over to the agency, leaving Stephanie with Josh.

"Mr. Pierce, what are you doing here so late?" the security guard asked as he and Connie approached the entrance to the agency.

"Late, it is only eight o'clock, Gloria. How's business tonight?" Davin said as he ran his badge through the scanner. Connie followed Davin and ran her badge through the scanner.

"Just have to check a couple of things up in the office," Davin replied as he and Connie walked past Gloria.

When they reached Davin's office, he picked up the file he needed to read and sat down behind his desk. "Hell, this can't be good."

"What can't be good?" Connie asked as she sat across from him in the overstuffed chair.

"Close the door, so we can discuss this. Your clearance level is high enough for this." Davin replied.

"What is it, babe?"

"This is the report that I was waiting for most of the day; it is the briefing for the President as to the state of the country. It says here that the country is healing, but it will take some time. It goes on to say that North Korea is increasing the number of troops on the 38th parallel, that can't be good. But what I am looking for is not in this report," Davin said and then continued to look at the paperwork on his desk, "Here it is." Reading down the page, he finally found what he was looking for; but before he could tell Connie, there was a knock on his door. He looked at Connie, who stood and opened the door.

"Hello Joanne, long time, please come in," Davin said when he looked up and saw Joanne Morgan standing at the door. "What are you doing here?"

"Hi Davin. Heard you were in the building and wanted to talk to you for a minute, may I?" Joanne Morgan asked.

"Sure, please, this is my wife Connie, Connie this is Joanne Morgan, our North Korean agent," Davin introduced them. "What's on your mind?"

"Can we talk in front of your wife?" Joanne asked.

"Yes, as long as you don't go over too high. Connie is one of our newest field agents."

"Good, well I am no longer your North Korean field agent. Kind of got compromised and their Commander of Secret Police gave me a warning that if I step foot in North Korea, she would have me arrested as a spy and over there the only penalty of being a spy is death after a long spell of being tortured, which may kill you before the firing squad does."

"So what has Ashley got you tasked to do now that you are not part of the North Korean project?" Davin asked

"Well, that is what I need to talk to you about, I was hoping that you might find another spot in Covert Operations where I can use the training I have."

"Technically you have been in Covert Ops; true, you reported to Ashley directly, but that was because she used to be Director of Covert Ops before becoming the big boss. She had decided that until you were off the North Korean assignment, she would remain your controller."

"Okay, so what is my assignment, Mr. Pierce?" Joanne asked.

"I don't know just yet. But rest assured I will have an answer for you by close of normal business tomorrow. I need to discuss this with Josh, ah, Mr. Randal, and you know he is in the hospital. I do have a few ideas and will discuss it with him and will have a good spot for you."

"Good, I will stop by tomorrow before normal close of business," Joanne said.

"Is there anything else you want to tell me?"

"Yes, there is one more thing. I was contacted by Soon-Bok Kim, you know who she is."

"Yes, know her very well, go on."

"She kidnapped me, but not in the normal sense of a kidnap. She took me to a coffee shop and wanted to talk to me about a deal, a deal that would expose the mole we have in our agency. She only asked for one thing and she would give us the name of the mole and copies of everything that was compromised. I discussed this with Ashley and we made the deal."

"What did she want?" Davin asked.

"She wanted to know the location of General Shin. We gave it to her and then she killed him. Guess you heard about that," Joanne stated.

"Yeah, in the report from Polson, Secret Service; he was working with one of our teams in Cannes. She was given free access; we kind of knew what she was going to do, but was asked not to interfere. His death also stopped any possible way of finding out who paid him to launch those missiles."

"I don't know about that; you will find out soon, so I will just spill the beans. It seems that the Nazi commander, one Gregory Dietrich is a multi-millionaire and financed the entire operation to take Washington D.C.; he also let it be known that he paid Shin to launch those missiles. He is a talker, feeling like he deserves credit for exposing our vulnerabilities. He is happy about it, and said he would do it again if he had the chance. This report is pretty complete; Mr. Dietrich is a fanatic with a death wish. And he will get his wish pretty soon," Joanne reported.

"Wow, so all this was done by one sick Nazi fanatic."

"Well, yes, and no. He is the grandson of a very famous Nazi from World War II," Joanne said and continued to report what she had found out.

"An old time Nazi fanatic; just what we need in today's world. Davin will it ever end in world peace and good will to everyone?" Connie piped in.

"I guess, Joanne, this is not the end," Davin stated and then closed the report he had on his desk. "

www.ingramcontent.com/pod-product-compliance
Lightning Source LLC
Chambersburg PA
CBHW062129170626
46813CB00002B/625